WILLIAM THE CONQUEROR: NOWHERE TO HIDE

CAROLINE CORBY was born and brought up in London. She studied mathematics and statistics at Bristol University, then became a banker and spent thirteen years in the City, ending up as a director in a venture capital company before deciding to leave her job to spend more time with her young family.

Caroline has always enjoyed history and wanted to find a historical novel aimed at children that would capture her daughters' imagination. After searching without success, she decided to write one herself and the Before They Were Famous series was born. It explores the early lives of some of history's most fascinating characters, who, in shifting, dangerous worlds, struggle to make their mark and become heroes of the future. Of *William the Conqueror: Nowhere to Hide*, Caroline says: "I was amazed to discover that William's life was under threat throughout his childhood. It must have been terrifying for him."

Caroline lives in Hampstead, North London, with her husband and three daughters, aged fifteen, thirteen and eleven.

Other titles in the series

CAROLINE CORBY

WILLIAM THE CONQUEROR

NOWHERE TO HIDE

WALKER
BOOKS

First published in 2009 by Walker Books Ltd
87 Vauxhall Walk, London SE11 5HJ

2 4 6 8 10 9 7 5 3 1

Text © 2009 Caroline Corby
Cover design © 2009 Walker Books Ltd
Boy on horse image © Image Source/ Getty Images

This book has been typeset in Usherwood and Tempus.

Printed in Great Britain by Clays Ltd, St Ives plc

British Library Cataloguing in Publication Data:
a catalogue record for this book is
available from the British Library

ISBN 978-1-4063-1372-7

www.walker.co.uk

For Dan

PART I

FALAISE CASTLE, NORMANDY
DECEMBER 1034

1

"CHIN up, William. Look proud. Your father will call you at any moment."

William was waiting with his mother in a corridor outside two impressive oak doors. One was ajar and beyond it he could see a large hall, crowded with people dressed in their finest robes. There were earls in chainmail, bishops in purple cassocks and barons in wool cloaks lined with fur. William had never seen so many of the grand families of Normandy in one place, and in the middle of winter too.

On Duke Robert's orders, all had journeyed across the frozen countryside, summoned to a council at the great castle of Falaise. But what could possibly be so urgent? William and his mother had only just had time to change from their muddy travelling clothes before they were hurried upstairs by the elderly castle warden saying, "Madam, thank goodness you've come. The duke's been frantic."

"We came as soon as we were sent for," said Herleve.

"You know the duke, ma'am," the man answered wearily. "When he gives an order, soon is not quick enough."

"Why *is* everybody here?" William asked, once the warden had gone to let the duke know of their arrival.

"You'll find out soon. Now, are you ready?" asked his mother.

Herleve Fulbert was a petite woman. She wore her dark hair swept back into a single plait that reached below her waist, her nose was delicately turned up and her skin was as pale as a candle. She frowned with concentration as she ran a searching eye over her son.

He was a boy of eight years, tall for his age, with a freckled face, straight russet hair and an air of seriousness which was reinforced by the formality of his clothes – a pale green tunic embroidered with silver thread at the collar and cuffs, and brown britches with matching felt shoes. A tiny sword hung from his waist. After shaking out a last crease, Herleve said, "I suppose you'll do. When you're called, walk as grandly as you can to the stage at the back of the hall. Don't smile at anyone. Don't even catch anyone's eye. Do you understand?"

"Of course. You've already told me."

"But this is important. Tonight you must do as I say."

William was not surprised by his mother's fretting; she was always anxious at court, for Herleve was the daughter of a tanner, a man engaged in the grubby business of turning hides into leather. William's father, Duke Robert, was only nineteen when, returning from a hunt, he saw her washing linen in a river and was instantly smitten. His nobles had never forgiven Herleve for her humble origins, or for having William, the duke's only child, out of wedlock. Although they didn't dare show their distaste for "Miss Fulbert" in the presence of the duke, his mistress wasn't spared when he was out of earshot. William had heard his mother called a "witch" and a "peasant". It was only at Roche, the manor house Duke Robert had given her, that Herleve could live in peace.

William peeked again through the gap in the doors.

"When will the meeting start?" he asked his mother, rubbing his hands to warm them, for the castle's stone walls did little to keep out the bitter December wind.

Herleve ruffled her son's hair affectionately.

"I know it's a long wait for someone who's only eight, but you must be patient. The duke will call you soon enough."

William was even more puzzled. Why would his father call him in front of all these grand people and would he have to go in alone?

"You'll come with me, won't you?" he asked.

Herleve shook her head.

"No, it's you, and not me, that must be seen today."

It was the answer William expected. On his last two visits to Falaise his father had gone out of his way to ensure that he was rarely seen with his mother. At banquets Herleve ate alone in her room and she hadn't shared the same pew at mass. William suspected the duke, like his nobles, was ashamed of her and it troubled him. He couldn't think what she'd done to deserve such treatment.

A trumpet salute brought his attention back to the hall. His father was on the wooden stage.

"My Lords," the duke announced in a voice that carried easily across the hall, "I have gathered you here today for a council, for I have important news."

The duke was a giant of a man with hair as red as his son's. He always dressed as though he were about to go into battle: heavy chainmail, a sword swaying from his belt and spurs on each ankle. All knights wore spurs, but his were by far the most magnificent in the room – solid gold spikes with letters engraved along the length of them. As he paced confidently round the stage they made a pleasant clunking sound and glinted in the torchlight.

"After years of war," Duke Robert continued, "the duchy is at last at peace with itself and its neighbours. In the west, Brittany has signed a truce. To the south and east, France is our loyal friend. It is now time for me to take care of my soul. I will shortly be leaving Normandy on a pilgrimage to Jerusalem where I will beg forgiveness for my sins."

William knew the sin everyone would be thinking of. Eight years ago, when Robert's father died, he had fought with his elder brother, Richard, for control of Normandy. After being badly defeated and pleading for mercy from Richard, he then held a banquet to celebrate their reconciliation. That night Duke Richard died of a mysterious stomach complaint and so Robert inherited the duchy after all. Everywhere it was whispered that Robert had poisoned Richard.

Since then, Duke Robert had crushed his enemies, brutally slaughtering men, women and children, but maids gossiped that it was the murder of his own brother that haunted him and left him pacing his rooms night after night, unable to sleep. It would explain his decision to abandon Normandy and ride across Europe to the mysterious Holy Land. The journey would take at least a year and would be fraught with danger from bandits and disease. The venture was madness, unless Duke Robert couldn't live without the peace it would bring.

"Brother, when do you depart?" It was Lady Alice, the duke's sister and William's aunt, who broke the stunned silence. She was a short, dumpy woman who looked swamped by her elaborate dress and jewellery. Every podgy finger sparkled and a long gold chain hung to her waist.

"In a month," the duke replied.

There was a rumble of displeasure and an austere man, dressed all in black and standing at the back of the hall, raised his hand. His left eye was missing, giving him a lopsided appearance.

"Who's that?" whispered William to his mother.

"Lord Gacé. After your father, he's the most powerful man here. He owns acres and acres of land. Listen to what he has to say."

"Your Grace, you're a young man," declared Gacé. "A

pilgrimage can wait, but the duchy can't. If you leave, anarchy will return."

"I'll only be gone for twelve months," answered the duke. "Surely my knights can behave for that long."

A ruddy-faced man stepped forward to speak.

"That's Lord Cotentin, isn't it?" whispered William, remembering him scoffing plates piled high with food at the Easter feast.

"That's right," said his mother, looking pleased. "You're learning. Cotentin's from western Normandy. He's Lord Gacé's bitter enemy."

William studied the two men. They couldn't have been more different. Where Gacé was bony with a gaunt face, Cotentin was beefy with wobbling chins. Gacé was dressed soberly whereas Cotentin looked like a peacock, his generous stomach squeezed into a bright ruby-red robe.

"Your Grace, the threat could come from outside Normandy," Cotentin warned. "Our enemies could take advantage of your absence, particularly since you have no heir."

The duke glared. "Why do you say I have no heir? You will see him for yourself." He raised his voice. "William, come here!"

William was so surprised he didn't move. His father couldn't possibly mean it. All his life he'd assumed that one day the duke would give up his mistress and marry a grand lady, and a child from that union would inherit the rich Duchy of Normandy. Yet here he was being called in front of all these powerful men.

Herleve gave her son a gentle push. "Go on," she whispered, "and remember what I said."

The white-haired warden opened the doors. William set his shoulders back and, swallowing hard, walked into the crowded hall, knowing that his life had just changed forever.

AS he crossed the silent hall, William was acutely conscious of hundreds of hostile eyes watching him. Duke Robert was calling him "heir"! He was shocked, but what would they be feeling? His uncles, cousins and some of the more ruthless barons must think they had a better claim to the duchy, yet he'd been chosen. William hardly knew whether to thank his father or beg him to change his mind.

He tried to remember his mother's instructions. Resting his hand on his tiny sword, he climbed the four wooden stairs to the stage where his father was waiting. The duke picked him up and held him aloft.

"My son is fit and strong and no one has a more auspicious beginning. When he emerged from the womb he grabbed a handful of straw so tightly his midwife couldn't pull it from him. A priest told me it was a sign – that one day he will seize and hold great lands. Normandy will be safe with him as duke, for what greater prize could there be? Tonight, before all of you, I declare William as my heir and your liege lord. Every person here is a witness to this deed. Is anyone unhappy with what I propose?"

The duke's deep voice rumbled menacingly round the chamber. Only an ancient archbishop dared speak.

"Your Grace, as a man of the church I can only applaud your desire to undertake such an arduous pilgrimage, but even I must beg you to think of the duchy. William looks like a fine boy but a child cannot rule Normandy. Your journey will be gruelling and there is no guarantee of your safe return. We must have a ruler or there will be chaos."

There was a murmur of agreement.

"Archbishop, don't worry. I have already appointed two guardians for my son," answered the duke. "The first is my most loyal knight, Count Gilbert of Brionne. He will rule the duchy as regent until either I return or my son reaches maturity. The second is my steward, Osbern of Chambrais. He'll be responsible for William's safety and will be constantly at his side. Gentlemen, come here."

William gazed curiously at these strangers. Osbern was the duke's most senior steward. He was in his fifties, a plainly dressed man with pockmarked skin and thinning hair, who had devoted his life to managing Duke Robert's estates, overseeing the hundreds of pages, grooms, washerwomen, cooks and serving girls necessary to the functioning of a castle. He climbed slowly up the stairs. Gilbert was ten years younger and much more vigorous. He was expensively dressed in chainmail and an azure robe and was tall and heavy-set with the thick neck of a warrior. He had tousled, flaxen hair, ruddy cheeks and such a friendly expression that William instinctively warmed to him.

"On the way to Jerusalem," continued the duke, "I'll leave my son in Paris in the care of my overlord, King Henry of France. I ask again, is anyone unhappy with these arrangements?"

William had a mad, desperate urge to shout, "Yes, me!" He had no wish to be carted off from Normandy, a land that his Viking ancestors had conquered a hundred years before from neighbouring France, but he knew it was hopeless; once his father had made up his mind there was no changing it.

"Then I command each of you," said the duke, "to kiss the hand of my son and swear on the bones of Saint Ouen your loyalty and devotion to him."

The duke passed William a box. It was inlaid with gold, rubies and pearls and contained a precious relic – the finger of Saint Ouen, the founder of one of the greatest abbeys in Normandy. An oath taken on such a sacred object was binding, for anyone who broke it risked their soul.

The one-eyed Lord Gacé was the first up the wooden steps. William held out his hand and felt rough lips brush against his skin and then, holding the ornate box, Gacé recited the oath of allegiance. Next was Lord Cotentin, and then his two new guardians, Count Gilbert and Steward Osbern. They were followed by so many nobles that William could scarcely keep track. Some were tall, some short, some looked grand, others more ordinary, but to William they all had one disconcerting thing in common – a barely discernible, but nevertheless evident, lack of enthusiasm. He couldn't help feeling that, without his father's presence, none would willingly be making this promise.

William's arm soon ached but he held it high and firm, determined to show these men that he *was* worthy of the honour being bestowed on him. He desperately wanted to believe Duke Robert's faith in him was justified, but as each grim oath was extracted, his doubts returned – how would he ever be a match for his magnificent and daring father, and if he wasn't, how could he possibly rule these men?

Near the end of the queue came a studious-looking boy with dark, darting eyes and surprisingly fair hair. He was dressed in the rough, brown cloth of a holy man despite being only a few years older than William.

The boy fell to his knees, took the relic and said fervently, "I swear before God that I will serve you as long as I live." As he stood up he whispered, "Good luck, I'll do anything I can to help."

After the subdued words of the others, William was surprised by how grateful he was for this encouragement.

"Who are you?" he whispered back.

"Nicholas of Fecamp – your cousin."

William studied the boy more closely. So this was his

father's hidden nephew, son of the poisoned Richard, who'd been banished to a monastery at just three years old. Evidently Robert must have thought it prudent to summon him to Falaise, for his claim to the duchy was strongest of all. But judging by his words, Normandy was the last thing Nicholas wanted.

"How long are you here?" William asked.

"The duke's ordered me back to the abbey first thing in the morning. I'll leave before dawn."

William was disappointed. He was curious to learn more of the mysterious Nicholas but already another nobleman was waiting to take his turn and so, frustratingly, he had to let his cousin go and rejoin the crowd below.

"William, it's late," said the duke when the final oath had been taken. "The warden has put your things in the East Tower. Go to your room and get some rest."

The East Tower was the grandest part of the rambling castle of Falaise. It was where the duke had his own rooms and private chapel. So far William had always slept in the castle hall on his occasional visits to court and he had no idea which way to go. He paused at the doors, wondering who to ask for directions, when he caught a fleeting glimpse of a fair boy in a brown, sackcloth robe at the far end of a draughty corridor. Nicholas! He was only moments ahead of him. He *would* get the chance to talk to him after all.

William hurried along the stone passage, chasing after his cousin, but by the time he reached the end the boy was gone. *Which way?* thought William. A staircase on his left led down to the store rooms and kitchen; the one on his right up to a large guard room with a roaring fire. Nicholas must be heading there for the night.

William hurried up the steep, spiral steps, determined to catch him, but after only a few turns the sound of urgent whispers from the stairs above brought him to an abrupt halt.

"... the boy has Osbern and Gilbert," a low, male voice was saying. "We can't take them both on."

"I agree they're a formidable team, but it means nothing," said another voice, deeper and more abrasive. "Whatever was said or done this evening was a farce."

"You can't mean that," said the first. "Remember, we all swore on Saint Ouen's bones."

"A vow unwillingly given, forced out, counts for nothing. Remember the blood of a tanner flows in his veins. It's an insult to Normandy! Once the duke's gone, loyalties will soon switch. That child's a low-born bastard who'll never amount to a thing..."

So that's what they think, thought William, as he crept back down the staircase, giving up on catching Nicholas. It was just as he'd suspected – they *did* despise him. It was so unfair. He couldn't help who his mother was and he didn't care. Why should he feel ashamed of her? She was kind and gentle and loyal to Robert. *The only thing I can do is show them they're wrong,* he thought. *They'll see. I'll be a duke no one will ever forget.*

FALAISE CASTLE – JANUARY 1035

"MOTHER, why can't you come to Paris?"

It was bad enough being sent to France, a land he'd never visited, to be left in the hands of a king he'd never met, without having to leave his family behind as well.

Herleve was meticulously folding the last of William's shirts, her long, ropelike plait dangling over a shoulder. She stopped and looked at her son who was dressed in travelling clothes – woollen britches, a brown tunic tied at the waist and a heavy cloak that dragged along the floor but which he could wrap round himself to keep out the chill wind on the long ride ahead.

"You can't live the rest of your life in a woman's household," she explained gently. "I know you're young, but your father's chosen this path for you. He wants you to learn the ways of a knight."

"But why Paris? Why can't I stay here with Gilbert?"

"As regent, Gilbert will be busy ruling Normandy, and you must pay homage to the French king. The peasants swear to serve their barons, the barons to serve the knights, the knights take an oath to serve the duke and the duke to serve the king. It's a chain. If any link is missing, we're all weaker. You know that."

"But I could do that and then come home. I won't know anybody there," said William. He knew he was whining, but now that his departure was almost upon him, he couldn't help it.

"Don't worry. Osbern will take care of you," answered Herleve reassuringly. "He's a good man. I've seen the way he looks after the servants on the duke's estates. He's fair and reasonable."

"But he's so much older than me."

"That's why Guy's going too. Lady Alice is packing his bags right now."

Vicomte Guy of Burgundy was Lady Alice's only son. At ten, he'd already begun his knighthood training. He excelled at hunting, playing the lute and chess. In fact, by his own account, Guy excelled at everything. He could be tiresomely conceited – grandly insisting on being served first at supper, but whenever he caught William's eye he'd wink, as if it were all a joke. Overall William was glad he was coming to Paris but surprised Lady Alice was letting him go. Over the years she'd made her feelings plain about "vulgar" Herleve and her "bastard" son and what she thought of her brother, the duke's, "degrading liaison".

"Now you're the heir, you'll see lots of things like that will change. Many people will want to be close to their future duke," William's mother had explained on hearing the unexpected news.

"I think you have everything," said Herleve, putting a final pair of stockings into a leather saddlebag. "It's almost time for you to leave but first there's something I must tell you." She glanced round the bare room, her blue eyes troubled and then lowered her voice to a whisper. "Whatever lies ahead, remember, my family will always be loyal to you. If you ever need help, you must come to us first. Your father's side of the family is more complicated and you should be wary of them. They all have ambitions of their own. Even though you are only a boy, you must try to think like a man and always be on your guard."

There was a knock at the door.

"Miss Fulbert, it's time," a servant called out. "They're waiting in the bailey."

"So soon!" said Herleve, looking startled. For a moment she hugged her son tightly and then gave him his bag and pushed him away. "You must go, William. Good luck."

Twenty packhorses were lined up in the bailey, the large, grassy courtyard enclosed by the castle's high stone walls. Over the next twelve months these animals would trek over a thousand miles, from Normandy to Paris, where William would be left, and then on through the Alps with Duke Robert and across the straits of Constantine on the long journey to Jerusalem.

William climbed up onto a grey mare. He was leaving Normandy, his home and his family, and he had no idea when he would be back.

PARIS – FEBRUARY 1035

"DO you see it?" asked Duke Robert.

William shaded his eyes from the afternoon winter sun, eager to take in every detail. For the last ten days the Normans had been following a busy bridle track. At first the land had been densely forested, then scrubby, and at last they had entered a lush plain with the great River Seine at its centre. The trail followed the Seine closely, gently twisting and turning through fertile land and marshes until finally they arrived at this collection of towers and steeples, the largest town in France and King Henry's capital – Paris.

The tallest buildings, where Henry had his castle, were on two islands in the middle of the river. On either bank were hundreds of houses crowded together, a cluster of church spires and the solid stone walls of a monastery. A stream of boats rowed between the islands and the two shores.

"Let's get going!" shouted the duke, kicking his horse hard in the flank. "With luck, we'll be there by sunset."

* * *

That first evening in Paris, Osbern took special care with William's clothes. On clean straw he laid out a crimson robe of the finest lambswool, embroidered with gold thread at the hem, plus stockings and criss-crossing garters. Finally, William stepped into slippers closed with thongs made from the softest kid leather.

"You've done well, Osbern" said the duke. "He's perfect. Let's go. We mustn't keep the king waiting."

They entered a magnificent banqueting hall, its high ceiling painted indigo with gold stars that glistened in the torchlight. The walls were hung with tapestries and at either end of the chamber were two huge roaring fires. The room was crowded with French knights who separated to the left and right when the Normans appeared, creating an aisle from the doorway to the throne where King Henry was reclining.

The king was olive-skinned with high cheekbones and a dark beard cut to a point. His garments were lined with ermine and his gold crown was encrusted with jewels. To William, he looked just as a sovereign should – noble, handsome and tough.

Duke Robert fell to his knees and kissed both of Henry's feet.

"Your Majesty, I am leaving for the Holy Land. In preparation, I have left Normandy to my son, William. I ask that you receive his oath of allegiance, as you received mine."

Henry stood up with outstretched arms.

"Get up, Robert, and greet me as a friend should."

The two men embraced. Although the duke was dressed in only the simple grey tunic of a pilgrim, his golden spurs and fine weapons left behind in Falaise, when the two men stood side by side they appeared to be equals, not supplicant and master. King Henry had come to the throne only four years earlier after a bitter struggle with his own brother. Duke Robert's help had been decisive in securing his victory, and both men knew it.

The king turned to William. "This must be your boy."

Something about Henry's expectant eyes calmed William and without a quiver in his voice he managed to pronounce loudly and clearly the words that Osbern had drummed into him over the last week.

"Your Majesty, I swear that from this day forward I will serve and be loyal to only you and your heirs."

He bowed and kissed the king's hand.

"William, I accept you as my vassal, and I will do everything in my power to protect you and your property," replied Henry, taking a leafy twig and a palm-sized clod of grass from behind his throne. "These gifts are symbols that signify that although I am your overlord, I grant you freedom in your lands."

William took the twig and the grass and held them aloft to cheers from the Norman knights. After his father, he was now their lord and the King of France himself had guaranteed his safety. For the first time since he'd left

Normandy, William felt that his time in France would turn out all right. King Henry seemed friendly enough. William would be in Paris for only twelve months and would then return home with his adventurous father who would protect him from those miserable nobles until he was ready to assume the duchy himself.

Little did he dream that in less than twelve months his father would be dead and, at the age of nine, he would become Duke of Normandy.

Part II

Reims, Eastern France
February 1040

WILLIAM was galloping out of the forest when he noticed four strangers approaching Reims, the most easterly castle in France. Their leader, a knight judging from his fancy armour, pulled up his horse at the ditch that circled the fort and jumped down, signalling for his men to wait. It was this that caught William's eye. Why didn't they carry on along the muddy track to the castle gates like other travellers?

"Hey Guy, slow down!" William shouted over his shoulder to his cousin who was at his heels and catching up fast.

As the only Norman boys at King Henry's court, William and Guy spent almost every day together. They'd expected to be in France for a year, but Duke Robert's calamitous pilgrimage had changed all that. On his return from Jerusalem the duke had fallen terribly ill. He'd rallied sufficiently to be carried homewards in a litter, but four years ago William received the news he dreaded: the fever had killed his father. The duchy was his.

William assumed he would go home immediately, but his guardians and King Henry decided he was safer in

France. He was too young to govern, so what possible good could he do in his turbulent homeland? King Henry would ensure he learnt the skills necessary for a ruler, Osbern would tend to his daily needs and Gilbert would settle any disputes amongst the nobles of Normandy. Only when they judged that the boy was old enough to assume his responsibilities would he return. And so year after year William stayed in France, with Guy as his companion.

Guy's horse was now neck and neck with William's.

"Afraid you're going to lose?" he taunted.

William tugged his reins and slowed down to a trot. "No. Let's say you won. Who do you think that is?" He pointed to the distant knight.

"No, not 'Let's say you won'," said Guy. He was a short, stocky boy with fair colouring and a classic, aristocratic Norman face – a high forehead, long, straight nose and prominent cheekbones. "I beat you, fair and square, *and* you started before me."

William and Guy were racing home from a boar hunt. They often tracked these fierce wild animals – the perfect sport for getting fitter and stronger and for perfecting their fighting technique. Much of this morning, however, had been frustrating. They'd circled through the woods, crossing their own tracks several times but finding nothing. Then, just when they were on the point of giving up, the hounds yowled and, after a brief chase, cornered a snarling hog. While it pawed the ground, ready to charge,

William had speared it through the neck, sending a spray of blood across the frosty ground. He'd loved it – the pursuit, the danger and the fact that he'd beaten Guy to the kill.

"Without doubt you beat me and I am the loser," William said, smiling good-naturedly. Admitting his cousin had won might stop him sulking over the boar and the thing that was really bothering Guy – William's investiture.

Ever since New Year, when King Henry of France had announced his intention to knight William, Guy had been irritable. He hated to be left out of anything and to make matters worse he was two years older. Osbern, William's loyal steward, had explained again and again that William was only being honoured at the young age of thirteen because he was a duke, but this had done little to appease Guy. William hoped that after tomorrow, when the ceremony was over and there were no more visitors, costume fittings and rehearsals, Guy would put it behind him and things would return to normal between them – an easy friendship that had sustained him through the long years in France.

"Glad you see the race my way," said Guy. "Now, what did you see?"

William pointed. "I reckon that knight's waiting for Osbern."

"Why do you think that?"

"Well, for one, he doesn't look French." Even from this

distance they could see the knight had a shock of fair curls. "And for another, something's up. Osbern's fretting, but he won't say why."

Over the years, William had grown fond of his steward. He appreciated his tact, diplomacy and dedication, and he was certain if Osbern was fussing, it would be on his account.

"It's your knighthood, that's all. It's sending everyone into a frenzy. That man will just be another guest for the illustrious event," said Guy resentfully.

"I don't think so. There's more to it than that."

Just then the castle door swung open and Osbern, dressed in a plain brown robe, began climbing down a wooden ladder. The only entrance to the stone keep was one storey above the courtyard, making it easier to defend but awkward to get in and out of. Osbern descended cautiously, feeling for one step and then the next. At last, he dropped out of sight behind a wooden fence that encircled the fort and then reappeared a few minutes later, hurrying along the path in the direction of the stranger as fast as his stiff leg would allow.

"I told you," said William triumphantly. "Let's find out what's going on. He must have news from Normandy."

They tied their horses to the nearest tree and raced to catch Osbern up, reaching him just a few feet from the stranger.

"Ah, I'm glad you're here, William. You have a visitor," said the steward.

"Do you bring a letter from my mother?" asked William.

Herleve occasionally sent messages to her son. She'd told him of her marriage to a squire called Herluin and of the birth of Odo, a baby boy.

"No, not from Lady Herleve, your Grace. It's news I must deliver in private."

The knight waved his three men away and then glanced meaningfully at Guy, indicating he would not speak in front of him. *But that's not necessary*, thought William. For the last five years he and Guy had shared rooms, food, horses and swords, and Guy was his cousin. Anything said to him could be said to Guy as well.

"Don't worry. You may speak freely," he said.

"I can't, your Grace," replied the stranger firmly. "This concerns Normandy."

"Norman business is my business too," said Guy huffily. "You can't know who I am – I'm Vicomte Guy of Burgundy, son of Lady Alice, nephew of the late duke and cousin of the present."

"I know," said the stranger, unimpressed by Guy's list of grand relatives, "but my message is for the duke and Osbern and nobody else, no matter how exalted they might be."

There was something about the commanding way in which the stranger spoke that stopped William from protesting at his impertinence.

"Guy, check the squires have the boar," he said quickly.

"I'll come as soon as I can."

With a face like thunder, Guy stalked off.

"That boy should learn to say 'Yes, Your Grace' to his duke," remarked the stranger coolly.

"That boy is my cousin and friend," answered William defensively.

Here in France, with the exception of his impending knighthood, the fact that he was duke and Guy was not made little difference. It would feel absurd and artificial to demand to be addressed by his title when Guy felt more like an older brother. And why was this stranger stirring things up that were none of his business?

"Who *are* you?" asked William petulantly.

"Surely you remember me, your Grace?" asked the man with a quizzical smile.

William shook his head.

"I'm Count Gilbert of Brionne, your guardian. I've come all the way from Rouen."

William was astonished. When he'd left for Paris, Gilbert had remained in Normandy as regent ruling the duchy in his absence, and William hadn't seen him since. All he remembered from that evening at Falaise Castle long ago when Duke Robert had nominated William heir was a hearty knight with a kind face. Now Gilbert looked much older, his fair hair turning to grey round his temples and his ruddy face drained by the endless, fruitless quest to bring peace to the duchy.

"Why have you come?" asked William.

"It's time for you to return home, Your Grace."

"To Normandy?"

"Yes. Five years is a long time for a duke to be absent."

William was lost for words. He'd spent so long in France it felt like home and King Henry had become like a father to him.

"When do you want the boy to come?" asked Osbern, as surprised as William.

"As soon as possible."

"But he's far too young."

"Osbern, he's about to be knighted," said Gilbert impatiently. "The news has reached Rouen. The court's saying if he's old enough for that, he's old enough to return. He can't stay here forever, and look at him. He's not a child anymore."

During his time in France, William had shot up. He was now over five and a half feet tall, towering over most men, with broad shoulders and limbs that were growing stronger every day. Already he could carry heavier armour than squires several years older than him and few could bend his bow.

"But is it safe? What about the rebellion?" said Osbern anxiously.

For many months reports of skirmishes between Gilbert and a band of nobles in the west of Normandy had been trickling through to France.

"That's the reason he's needed," explained Gilbert. "I can't quell this uprising unless the duke is there for people to rally round."

"Gilbert, you can't possibly ask King Henry to send William back to such chaos. You couldn't guarantee to keep him safe for a week."

William listened in silence as the two men argued back and forth. Osbern wanted to keep him out of harm's way in France until he was old enough to claim his birthright. Gilbert countered that if William didn't return soon there would be no duchy left to claim. Normandy would be broken into fragments by rebels, each grabbing what they could. William's homecoming was the only hope of uniting the duchy.

If the boy came, how would Gilbert propose to keep him safe? asked Osbern. Castle walls were useless against determined assassins. Had Gilbert really thought this through? The boy had been entrusted to their care and they had a sacred duty to ensure he reached maturity. Where better than in the peaceful land of France?

William waited for the two men to finish their discussion. Neither had thought to ask him his opinion and in truth he wasn't sure. France felt like home but Normandy was the land of his birth.

"Gilbert, I suppose if you're convinced, then I must be too," conceded Osbern at last. "You're in Normandy and I'm not. We must speak to the king tomorrow at the investiture breakfast, but I don't think he'll be easy to persuade."

"No doubt," said Gilbert grimly. "It must suit him to have the duke under his control. After all, the duchy originally belonged to France."

"That's not fair," interjected William.

Since the day his father had left, King Henry had provided him with the best tutors, horses, weapons and clothes, and tomorrow he was going to honour him with a knighthood. He'd treated William like a son. How dare Gilbert suggest that this was all a sham!

"William's right," said Osbern. "Gilbert, you've been immersed in Norman treachery for so long it's made you cynical. I only meant that the king will be concerned for his safety."

"I hope that's true," said Gilbert, "but tomorrow, we'll find out."

6

THE next morning Osbern fussed distractedly over the clothes he'd laid out on a richly embroidered quilt. He would have been anxious anyway about getting William ready for such a grand ceremony, but the extra worry of Gilbert's proposal was making him tetchy.

"Come on, William! Get in!"

Reluctantly, William pulled off his shirt and stepped into an uninviting tub of cold water. Guy was standing on a stool next to the barrel with a bucket in his hand. Despite the stool, he had to balance precariously on tiptoe to pour the pail of water over his taller, ganglier cousin.

"Guy, watch you don't splash the floor!" ordered Osbern.

Freezing water tumbled down.

"And another," said the steward.

William clenched his teeth as he was drenched again. He loathed washing, above all in winter when, despite roaring fires, the castle rooms were always damp and cold. Osbern insisted he do so every couple of months, but this wash was special – it was for the investiture and so Osbern was being particularly thorough.

Since William's return from the boar hunt, Osbern

had firmly taken charge of the final preparations for his knighthood. William was made to put on a simple gown and given no supper as traditionally he must fast. He'd passed a lonely night in an austere chapel with only the calls of the night watchman to mark the passage of time. He should have spent time in prayer, but he couldn't help returning again and again to Gilbert's news. What would Normandy be like? Where would he stay? Would he be reunited with his mother? And would he be safe? He was relieved when a priest appeared at dawn to hear his confession and bless his sword – at least it was a distraction. And finally here he was, washing away any sins, with the ceremony about to begin.

"And again!" ordered Osbern.

"I hate it," spluttered William, as he wiped water from his eyes. "That must be enough."

He was covered in goose pimples and shivering.

"Oh, for goodness sake, stop complaining," said Guy. "I'd willingly take your place."

"Guy," admonished Osbern sternly. "Not this again. We've been through it a hundred times already."

"Well, I still don't see why I can't be knighted at the same time. He's only thirteen and I'm fifteen and…"

"And he's the duke," interrupted Osbern. "You'd do well to remember that. William, come and get dressed. Guy, we'll see you in the courtyard."

Osbern passed William his clothes, handling each garment reverently: the white shirt for purity, the scarlet tunic for nobility and finally the black shoes and britches, reminders of the inescapability of death.

As William put on the sacred costume his apprehension returned. He was about to join the highest order in the land, an order whose tenets were faith, honour, courage and chivalry. Above all he could never again refuse a challenge nor turn from an enemy. It was a daunting prospect.

"And finally your sword," said Osbern, picking up an ornate silver weapon in a beautifully enamelled scabbard. "Now you're ready."

The entire French court was waiting in the castle bailey. Veiled ladies in gowns of pink, blue and green, men stamping their fur-lined boots against the bitter cold and, on the far side of the courtyard, King Henry, magnificently attired in chainmail, a crown and a bearskin cloak that skimmed the frozen ground.

It was early morning. The sky was a brilliant blue and the ground was crisp underfoot but William was oblivious to the cold.

"I come to you, your Majesty, to request that I be armed as a knight," he said as clearly as he could.

"For what purpose do you wish to join the order?" asked the king.

"To punish those who are evil, to protect the innocent and never to traffic with traitors," said William, reciting the age-old words.

"And will you serve me loyally?" boomed out Henry.

"I will. And will you in return protect me and my lands?"

"I will. As a sign of our allegiance, I dub you Sir William, Duke of Normandy."

With that King Henry pulled off a leather glove.

William braced himself, knowing he must do nothing to avoid what was coming. Next thing he knew he was reeling down onto the muddy ground, his cheek shockingly painful and the taste of blood in his mouth. King Henry had punched him hard on the left side of his face. It was the one and only beating William could receive from his suzerain and he must take it with courage and without retaliating. He'd watched many squires sit dazed on the ground after such a blow, but the most impressive were back on their feet in no time, whether their noses were bloodied or a tooth knocked out. William was determined to be one of these. Taking only a moment to check he could, he stood up, erect and steady, almost as tall as King Henry himself, to a rousing cheer.

The glittering spectators crowded in, passing him armour, piece by piece. First a coat of chainmail, then a shield and finally spurs sharpened to a point.

"By these, will all men know that William is now a knight," announced the king, "and that I am his overlord – his suzerain. Now let's go and celebrate. A feast awaits."

And at this feast, thought William, *my fate will be determined. Will I go home to Normandy or stay in France?*

EACH spring, Henry left Paris with his court to tour his kingdom. Over the years, William had grown familiar with the various castles they visited. Tours was beautiful, Mâcon was infested with bedbugs and the hunting at Roanne was second to none. But Reims William always loathed. It was damp, a constant wind blew across the plain and every room in the castle was depressing. The banqueting hall was no exception. Although their host, Baron Luc, had laid on lavish entertainment to celebrate William's knighthood – jugglers, a dwarf jester and minstrels strumming harps – it did little to cheer up the gloomy chamber.

"William and Guy, come here!" the king called from the high table. When they were seated he nodded in Gilbert's direction and added, "The regent of Normandy has come all the way from Rouen to see you knighted."

"Not just for that, your Majesty," explained Gilbert. "There is something I would like to discuss with you."

"Yes?" said Henry indifferently. "Well, first let us eat. This is William's celebration, remember."

A serving girl laid the table with a jug of ale, bottles of wine, bread, metal plates and a bowl of water. Once everyone had washed their hands and grace had been said, dishes of pheasant, deer and wild boar were brought from the kitchen, topped off by a final course of roasted peacock decorated with its own feathers.

William pulled a knife and spoon from his pocket but despite his day's fast and the delicious food, he had no appetite. His cheek was still stinging from the king's punch, but it was more than that. All he could think of as he pushed the meat round his plate was Gilbert's request and how Henry would respond. Gilbert and Osbern were similarly distracted, for they said little and Guy nothing at all, beyond muttering his congratulations. Only Baron Luc shamelessly flattered the king with one ingratiating comment after another – *How did his Majesty learn be such a marvellous rider? How was his bow so accurate? How did he stay so fit?* William couldn't wait for the meal to be over.

At last the dishes were cleared and King Henry said, "So, Count Gilbert, tell me, what's so important that you've made a visit to France?"

Gilbert wasted no time in outlining his proposal but as he spoke, King Henry's cheeks became flushed and his dark eyes flashed with irritation.

"You're asking me to send William into danger," he said angrily. "I won't do it! I swore I'd do what's best for the boy."

"Then allow him to leave with me, your Majesty," said Gilbert calmly but forcefully, as determined as the king to get his own way.

"How can it be in his interest to risk kidnapping, or murder? Normandy is in chaos. You're its regent. You must sort it out first."

"Your Majesty, Osbern and I, William's two guardians, are requesting you return the duke. You cannot deny us."

"You forget that his father left him with me," said the king in a tone which conveyed he would not be contradicted again. "William will not return until I say so. This is my final word. Boys, leave the table!" he added gruffly. "I need some peace."

"Now do you see you're trapped, your Grace?" whispered Gilbert to William, finding him some minutes later distractedly watching jugglers.

"I'm not sure," said William truthfully.

He hardly knew what to think. Was all his finery – the clothes, wall hangings, feather mattresses – really nothing but the trappings of a heavily disguised prison? Did the hours the king had spent instructing him in the arts of ruling, warfare and, most importantly, managing quarrelsome barons, count for nothing? When Henry called him "his Norman son", was it only a ruse to keep him in France? William couldn't believe it. The king was concerned with his safety. That was why he wouldn't let him leave. And yet what Gilbert had said nagged away at him.

"Well, I'm in no doubt," said Gilbert, "but I'm not finished yet. The king must be made to see that he cannot keep the Duke of Normandy at his court forever. One way or another, I'm going to get you out of here before it's too late."

8

"WILLIAM, come quickly!"

Guy was running across a ploughed field just outside the castle walls waving frantically.

Not now, thought William, standing with a gloved hand high in the air. Under the careful supervision of the court falconer, William was training a hawk. He put a finger to his lips – the bird must not be disturbed – but Guy took no notice.

"William, you must come. The king has given permission for you to leave. Osbern says we're to go first thing tomorrow, before he changes his mind."

So Gilbert has finally succeeded, thought William. For the last ten days he'd hounded the king, hinting that the Normans might come marauding into France if he did not return their duke, and now he'd got his way.

"Gilbert's incredible, isn't he?" said Guy as they hurried back to the castle. "Fancy managing to make the King of France change his mind. He's probably worried all Normans are as tough as Gilbert."

"Or Gilbert's convinced him he's right," said William.

"No, the king's scared. He knows we're warriors and the French aren't." After a pause he added, "Do you want to go?"

"I suppose so," William answered, "but it's been so long, I'll hardly know my own mother." Only yesterday he'd tried to picture her face. He remembered the long plait, and he thought her nose was straight and gently upturned at the tip, but he was conscious that his image of her was fading. "How about you?"

Guy shrugged. He hadn't seen his family in over five years.

"I don't know. It'll all be so different."

* * *

Early the next morning, when the sky was still grey, Henry accompanied William's small party of Osbern, Guy, Gilbert and his three Norman guards through the outskirts of Reims, a small town built in the shadow of the castle.

"I'm letting you go reluctantly," the king confessed to William as they rode side by side. "Gilbert has persuaded me that if you don't return you risk losing your birthright, and that's not something I want on my conscience, but never forget I am your suzerain. If you are ever truly in trouble, call on me. I will put France at your disposal."

"Thank you, Sire. I'll never forget what you have done for me," answered William sincerely.

"And remember, if you are ever in serious difficulty…"

"I'll come to you, I promise."

"Then good luck," said Henry, halting his horse at the last rickety house in the lane. "It won't be easy, but you're clever and brave. I believe you have the qualities of a ruler."

And with that he turned and rode away. William trotted on, but he kept glancing over his shoulder until Henry was gone. *I wonder if I'll ever see him again*, he thought sadly. Whatever Gilbert said about the king's motives for keeping him in France, William had no doubts. Henry *was* on his side. Leaving him felt like losing a second father.

* * *

Rain lashed across the marshes. After a long day in the saddle, everyone was soaked and exhausted. William's legs and arms were stiff and cold and his sopping red hair was sticking in clumps to his forehead. Despite his thick cloak and tunic he could feel chilly raindrops trickling down his back.

Finally, just as the sun was setting, Gilbert halted his horse at a wide bend in the River Avre.

"Your Grace, this is where we cross into Normandy."

William looked at the flat countryside that lay across the water. So this was where he would leave French territory and enter his duchy. His land looked bleak and uninviting and to make matters worse, this was the least glorious homecoming imaginable. When King Henry travelled around his kingdom he did so in style. A great procession rolled through the countryside, trumpeters announced his arrival in each village and he was showered with gifts of ham and wine. But there was no one to greet

William and anyway he was travelling in disguise. As they approached the border Gilbert had insisted it could be dangerous if they were recognized. Any markings that could identify them on either their shields or tunics must be covered until they reached the safety of Rouen. To William it felt as though he was slipping back into his own land like a thief.

That day and all of the next, the Normans rode north-west, following a muddy trail. The journey was grim. They were all tired and Osbern's stiff leg was particularly sore, sticking out awkwardly as he rode, his face grey and grimacing in silent pain. But the worst thing was the state of the countryside they were travelling through. Gilbert's men had recently recaptured it from the rebel barons, and the fighting had caused misery. Fields were unploughed and overgrown with weeds. Whole villages were burnt out and abandoned, the thatched roofs turned to cinders and the walls scarred with smoke.

The route was dotted with desperate people, squatting in makeshift tents. Round a bend in the track a little girl, not much older than five, was crouching in the shelter of a prickly hedge. She was dressed in muddy rags providing little warmth against the bitter wind, her cheeks were feverishly red and she seemed too young to be alone. As the horses approached, she held up her hand.

"Please, sirs, can you spare some food?"

Gilbert ordered one of his men to throw her some bread which she scrambled after, but to William it seemed pitifully little. *And this is in the east of Normandy, the area under Gilbert's control,* he thought. What condition would the far west be in, where war was still raging?

Riding side by side with Gilbert, William asked, "How are things in the west?"

"Difficult. It's always been the wildest part of the duchy, but as long as we have Cotentin and Gacé and now you, victory will eventually come."

William remembered the two lords – the larger-than-life, gregarious Cotentin and his opposite and rival, the serious and disciplined, one-eyed Gacé.

"Are they loyal?" he asked.

"I hope so," said Gilbert. "If your reign is to succeed, they must be."

They pressed on relentlessly, stopping only when the horses were too exhausted to continue. Finally, just as the mist cleared and a watery sun broke through the clouds, Gilbert pointed out the stone battlements of Rouen on the horizon. William's long journey was nearly over. After five years away the duke was almost home.

Rouen – March 1040

WILLIAM was still in his damp travelling clothes, warming his hands by the fire with Gilbert, when there was a commotion at the door and a guard appeared.

"It's your aunt, Lady Alice, your Grace. She wishes to see you as soon as possible."

Guy's mother pushed past him and strode in. Like her son she was short and, from the few stray hairs peeking out from under her severe wimple, fair, but there the similarity ended. Where Guy had an easy charm, Lady Alice stood on her dignity, her elaborate jewellery announcing her exalted position at court. She wasted little time on pleasantries.

"My dear nephew, thank God you're here. Gilbert has done his best as regent but..." she waved a glinting hand limply, as if to say his best was not good enough. "Now you're back in Normandy, surrounded by your family," she continued, "things will be easier. Perhaps a council should be established to advise you. What do you think, your Grace?"

William knew exactly what Lady Alice was up to. He'd only just returned and already she was manoeuvring for power. Clearly Rouen was going to be a snake pit, where he must find people he could trust, people who had nothing to gain. He instantly thought of the Fulberts – his mother's side of the family had never been part of the court.

"Aunt, give me time to consider your proposal," he said diplomatically, and then he turned to Gilbert. "Will my mother be here tonight?"

His guardian looked surprised.

"I'm sorry, your Grace, but Herleve Fulbert must not be seen anywhere near you."

"You forget who she is," William retorted, stung by Gilbert's words.

"And so should you, if you hope to be duke for long," interjected Lady Alice.

"You mean you won't let me see her at all?" William asked Gilbert, ignoring his aunt.

"Your Grace, I've spent five years trying to preserve your inheritance," explained his guardian wearily. "Things are difficult enough. You must understand how people feel about your mother. It's bad enough that their duke is a child, but a bastard as well … it's too much. You mustn't remind them. It's hard, but it must be so."

William didn't doubt that Gilbert was doing what he thought best but it was still a blow. He'd expected to be reunited with his mother that evening and now Gilbert was telling him he could never see her again. For the moment he had little choice but to obey, but silently he made a promise to himself – as soon as he was able he would find his mother, no matter what anyone said.

ROUEN – SEPTEMBER 1040

WILLIAM passed an uneasy summer at Rouen Castle. Much of the time Gilbert was away, fighting one exhausting campaign after another. The news from the west wasn't good, but as long as the rebels had no leader powerful enough to unite them, Osbern reassured William, it was not catastrophic. Still, William couldn't help pondering gloomily on what would happen if he were defeated. Banishment to the church like his cousin Nicholas was unlikely. Any man that declared himself duke would have to kill his rival.

To distract himself from his troubles William threw himself into physical activity, growing fitter and stronger every day. Each morning he rode through the fields and forests around Rouen, learning to control his horse with his knees, leaving his hands free to hold a shield and sword. After riding practice there was hunting, falconry, swordsmanship and lessons in battle tactics. Guy joined him whenever Lady Alice would let him for, since his return from Paris, she seemed determined to see as much of her son as possible.

"Gilbert wants to speak to you, your Grace," said a breathless page one grey autumn morning when William and Guy were heading off to the stable.

"Guy, go on without me," said William. "I'll catch up when I can."

As soon as he saw Gilbert, William knew there was trouble.

"Your Grace, you can't stay in Rouen anymore," said his guardian. "I've just received terrible news – Lord Cotentin has switched sides and is leading the rebellion. Vimoutiers Castle has already fallen. I'm leaving this afternoon to try and retake it. He must be stopped before he gets too strong."

"Can you defeat him?" William asked tentatively. He knew Cotentin owned vast tracts of land in the west and had many knights and soldiers at his disposal.

"I'll have to, or others will join him," said Gilbert, "but in the meantime you must move to somewhere that's easier to defend than Rouen."

"Where?" asked William.

"South, to Vaudreuil Castle. It's built on an island in the River Seine."

William's heart sank. A remote fortress, cut off from news of the fighting, was the last thing he wanted.

"Must I go?" he asked.

"Yes, your Grace. You leave tonight. There's not a moment to lose."

* * *

The sky was dark by the time William, Guy and Osbern climbed into a tiny rowing boat wobbling in choppy water.

"Thank God we're here," said Osbern. Gilbert had entrusted him with getting William to Vaudreuil safely and the responsibility weighed heavily upon him.

"Nowhere's secure anymore," he'd muttered several times on the journey. "If the duke is captured, what will become of us?"

"Watch out, the current's strong. Anyone who falls in won't be coming out alive," said the ferryman, grimacing, revealing a mouth with few teeth.

He heaved the oars into the inky-black river and began rowing. Their progress was almost imperceptible at first, but when they were halfway across the river they caught the current and, with the help of the tiller, the ferryman steered the boat to a jetty where a flight of steep steps had been carved into the rocks.

William stared up at the silhouette of the castle against the night sky. The fortress, which occupied the whole of the island, looked grim and uninviting. Despite the late hour not a single light could be seen flickering in any of its windows.

"Can we borrow your lamp?" asked Osbern.

"No, I need it," said the oarsman as he pulled away, leaving them alone on the jetty.

"Never mind," said the steward. "We'll find the way."

In the dark, they stumbled up the roughly cut, slippery steps, Osbern leaning heavily on William, and then along a gravel path until they were hit by a hideous stench.

"The cesspit," said Osbern. "It can't be far now."

They groped their way towards a large arch in the castle walls. Osbern banged hard on the solid wooden door.

"Come on, come on," he murmured to himself as he tried again.

"Who is it?" asked a gruff voice at the third time of knocking.

"Your duke," said Osbern. "Open up or there'll be trouble."

The door creaked open to reveal a soldier and, behind him, an elegant woman dressed in rich brocade. She had long dark hair which was parted at the centre and neatly plaited. Her face was pale but guarded.

"I'm Lady Gunnor, your Grace. It's an honour to have you here. Many apologies for not being more welcoming but you cannot be too careful these days."

Holding a flaming torch, Lady Gunnor led them through several gates and courtyards. As they walked, she pointed out the thickness of the walls, the invincibility of the keep and the large number of soldiers ready to defend them.

"My husband's family built this castle. When he left for a pilgrimage I swore I would preserve it for him. If he ever returns, he'll find it exactly as he left it."

They entered the grand keep, passing storage chambers

and guard rooms until they reached the Great Hall. At this late hour, it was full of people sleeping on a straw-strewn floor. Disturbing as few as possible, they followed Lady Gunnor to the far corner.

"This leads to your rooms, and only to your rooms," she explained as they trooped up a spiral staircase. "They're at the top of the North Tower, the safest part of the castle. Here it is."

Before them was a surprisingly large chamber with two narrow windows, a comfortable-looking four-poster bed and a wooden chest. A fire was burning brightly in the hearth.

"It should have everything you need – even your own privy."

Lady Gunnor walked across the room and pulled aside a thick curtain which hid a small cupboard-sized recess with a stone shelf in which a hole had been cut. "My husband thought of everything. This was his room, but you can have it until he returns as long as you look after everything. I don't want anything to be damaged. Osbern and Guy, your room is the last door we passed. It's directly below the duke's." She turned to William. "Your Grace, a guard will be outside your room, day and night. His name is Martin. You can trust him."

"I'd prefer to sleep in the Great Hall, with everyone else," said William.

It was what he'd been used to in Normandy and in France.

"That would be too dangerous. I cannot possibly vouch for everyone there. By day you may move around the castle freely, except for the monastery, of course, which is for the monks alone, but by night you are safest here. If you wish to leave the island you must inform me and I will arrange an escort. Your regent, Gilbert, was insistent on this point. He is most concerned about assassins. Now if you don't mind, Steward Osbern and Vicomte Guy, would you please come with me to oversee the unpacking?"

William was left alone in the grand room. He crossed over to the bed, pulled back one of the drapes that surrounded it and sat down. The mattress was stuffed with feathers and was beautifully soft. The sheets were linen and the blankets the finest wool. It was the most sumptuous room William had been in since his time in Paris but this was of little comfort. Gilbert had put him in this gilded cage because it was no longer safe for him to be outside. His situation was becoming more and more precarious and there was nothing he could do about it.

11

Vaudreuil – October 1040

WILLIAM woke at dawn. Curious, he went to the window, pushed open the wooden shutters and was amazed by what he saw. No wonder Lady Gunnor was so proud; Vaudreuil Castle was magnificent. It was built on a lump of rock in the centre of the River Seine and was much bigger than he'd realized the previous night, with two sets of stone fortifications, a vast keep and turrets. The outermost wall hugged the rocky cliffs so closely that it was impossible to imagine how its masons hadn't fallen to their deaths. Within this was an inner wall encircling a generous bailey, a grassy courtyard with a pretty chapel, a carpenter's workshop with piles of wood stored outside, a blacksmith's forge and many barns and outhouses. There were kennels for hunting dogs, livestock pens for pigs, sheep and goats, a chicken run, stables, dovecotes to provide pigeons for the table – and one large, austere building with few windows, presumably the monastery Lady Gunnor had mentioned. Finally, in the centre of the bailey was the main tower, a stone building three storeys high, with crenellations and lookout points beautifully cut from granite.

As William looked down, oblivious to the cold draught whistling round his legs, the castle came to life. Grooms, servants, washerwomen, craftsmen, cooks, falconers and dog-keepers began their first chores. A friar hurried across the courtyard to the chapel, late for morning prayers, whilst a young girl threw corn to a flock of chickens.

"Isn't it marvellous? Preserving it is my greatest responsibility." Lady Gunnor had come quietly into the room and was standing behind William gazing rapturously at her castle. She was dressed in green linen and around her hips hung a belt with an enormous ring of keys which chinked as she moved.

"Everything looks very orderly," agreed William, feeling rather ill at ease and a little ashamed to be caught in only a nightshirt.

"It is. I keep it that way. Ah look, here's the maid with your breakfast."

A sturdy girl came in carrying a tray with a mug of cider, a roll and a bowl of porridge. It was the first decent meal William had been offered since his flight from Rouen and, feeling famished, he reached out for the bread.

"Stop!" said Lady Gunnor, alarmed. "Your Grace, my instructions are that you mustn't eat anything until it's been tested. Constance, go ahead."

Obediently, the girl put the tray on a wooden chest and took a bite of bread and a sip of the cider, then dipped her finger into the gruel. Constance was solidly built, with wiry brown hair and a straight pointed nose that looked a little too big for her face. She had a small mouth which didn't quite close over two protruding front teeth. Watching her chew, William was reminded of a rabbit.

"Now we'll count to a hundred."

"This is absurd," protested William. "I'm in a fortress. Nobody can get to me."

"Not over the wall," said Lady Gunnor, "but there are other ways, your Grace. I must insist."

When she had finished counting, she turned enquiringly to Constance.

"I feel fine, my Lady," said the serving girl chirpily.

"Your Grace, you may eat. Constance will bring all your food and, each time, she will taste it, just as I've shown you."

The girl bobbed a curtsey and smiled. If he really had to be mollycoddled, William decided, she didn't seem such a bad sort to do it.

William returned to the monotonous routine he'd followed in Rouen. He went to church morning and evening, and during the day he practised duelling, swordsmanship and archery, usually with Guy.

Month after uneventful month passed and in all this time William rarely left the island. The efficient Lady Gunnor saw to that. If he wanted to hunt she insisted on him being surrounded by six horsemen at all times.

It made riding impossibly slow and so William stopped asking.

One day merged into another. Only the saint's days and occasional messages from Gilbert marked the passing of time. The siege against Cotentin was progressing slowly. His guardian had surrounded Vimoutiers and was bombarding it with catapults as well as trying to stop any food reaching the rebels, but surrender from starvation would take time – many horses were trapped inside and their flesh could be eaten.

"Thank God you're safe here," Osbern often remarked, but William knew he worried. The unspoken question was, what would happen if Cotentin were victorious? William tried not to think about it.

Autumn turned to winter and the days got cooler and bleaker. Snow blanketed the valley and the wind was bitter. It was too cold to spend much time outside, even in the more sheltered bailey, and so William and Guy had little to do except huddle in the Great Hall, playing cards or dice.

A week after lacklustre Christmas celebrations, they were sitting by a fire, bickering over who'd won a game of Nine Men's Morris when Osbern came in looking flustered. An important visitor had arrived.

"Who is it?'" asked William excitedly, for nobody had come for months.

"It's your English cousin, Prince Edward, your Grace."

Strange, thought William. He had a vague recollection

of a rather dreary old man with a love of scripture. *Why would Edward have travelled all this way?*

"What's he doing here?" he asked.

"Lady Alice brought him…"

"Really?" interrupted Guy, looking surprised.

"Yes," said Osbern, "and neither of you are fit to be seen. William, you must receive Edward. Guy, you must go to your mother. She's waiting for you in Lady Gunnor's room. But first you must both change or they'll be wondering what I've been doing with you."

"Shouldn't I go with William?" asked Guy. "Edward's my cousin too."

"No," said Osbern firmly. "He wants to see William alone and he doesn't have much time, so hurry."

"Why *has* Prince Edward come?" William asked again as they climbed the final stairs to the North Tower.

"For your blessing, I've heard," said Osbern. "He's to try his luck reclaiming the English throne. His brother's effort was a failure and he wants to make amends."

What can I offer? thought William despondently. He was barely in charge of his own duchy – how could he possibly help Edward win a faraway kingdom across the sea?

In no time Osbern found an azure velvet tunic and a matching cape lined with fur. "That's better. You must look the part. Remember, if he succeeds, Prince Edward will be King of England."

The prince was waiting in the Great Hall. He was a

gangly man in his forties with short, greying hair, a neat moustache and skin as pale as marble. When William entered, Edward came hurrying over.

"Your Grace," said the prince, speaking French fluently but with an accent that betrayed his foreign roots. "Normandy has sheltered me for twenty years since the Danes invaded England but finally I've been asked to return to London. The Danes are hated, their leader is weak and the English barons wish me to be their king. I've come here to seek your approval."

William was acutely conscious that Prince Edward was coming to him not as a boy, but as the Duke of Normandy. He stood as straight as possible, grateful for the fine clothes Osbern had found, and tried to imagine what his father would have done in the circumstances.

"Prince Edward, you have my blessing and that of Normandy too."

"Thank you, your Grace. I'm most grateful for the help that the duchy has given me, but the Danes will not give in easily."

Edward was asking for men. William knew he would look hopelessly weak if he offered him nothing.

"If you need soldiers, I will ask my guardian, Count Gilbert of Brionne, to send any he can spare."

"I will always be grateful, your Grace," said his cousin, kissing his hand, "and I will never forget the debt I owe you. I give you my word on that. With luck, my ship sails for England on the early morning tide. Lady Alice and her guards have graciously agreed to accompany me to Dieppe port. She has a castle there and tells me I can stay if the weather worsens."

"Is Lady Alice riding all the way to Dieppe?" asked William, surprised as the journey was a good sixty miles over rough land and his aunt was fond of her comforts.

"Yes. She's been most kind."

I wonder what she's after, thought William once Prince Edward had left. There must be an explanation for why she was prepared to ride from Rouen to here and then on to the coast, and it certainly wouldn't be to make sure Prince Edward had a restful stay at Dieppe. Could she be looking for a safe haven in England in case Normandy disintegrated, or did she have designs on becoming Queen of England? He wouldn't put it past her, for one thing was certain: Lady Alice never did anything without a reason.

"Oh, that woman!" said William out loud. "If only I knew what she was up to!"

"Can I help, your Grace?"

It was the maid, Constance, who was quietly brushing old straw into a pile on the far side of the hall. William hadn't noticed her slip in and was taken aback by her question. Since that first morning when Constance had tasted his food he'd seen her at every meal but he had hardly heard her say a word.

"I don't see how," he said huffily. "How would you know Lady Alice's plans?"

"I don't, of course, your Grace," said Constance quickly.

"But I might be able to help you find out."

William was torn between reprimanding her for her cheek, and curiosity. How did she think she could possibly help?

"What do you mean?" he asked guardedly.

"Lady Alice is with Lady Gunnor in her chamber right now, your Grace. I was cleaning it, but they sent me out, so they must have had something important to discuss. The room's very tall with a minstrels' gallery. I often have to show the musicians in. They tell me you can hear everything that's said from that balcony. Would you like me to take you to it?"

William was tempted. There was something about the cold, efficient way Lady Gunnor ran the castle that he found disconcerting. Like Lady Alice, her face was strangely blank, as if she didn't ever want to give away what she was truly thinking. If the two of them were together, maybe something was up.

"Are you sure they wouldn't know I was there?" he asked.

Constance smiled shyly. "I'm certain, your Grace. I know this place better than most; I've cleaned every corner."

She led William down a servants' staircase and through several stone cellars, pausing every now and then to check that no one was around.

They hurried through a series of underground granaries and a windowless buttery full of wine and beer before climbing a long, winding staircase.

"Here it is, your Grace," whispered Constance. "Tiptoe in and I swear they won't hear a thing."

William opened the door. Before him was a wooden gallery that overhung a double-height grand room – Lady Gunnor's private quarters. The balcony had a wool mat and several cushions. In the corner were three mandolins propped one against another, several trumpets, pipes and a single drum. The balcony was large enough to hold a troop of at least twelve musicians.

William slipped through the door and crawled forward. Lady Gunnor and his aunt must be right underneath him. He could hear their voices but he couldn't see either of them. He lay as still as he could and listened.

"Your castle will be quite safe, Lady Gunnor," Lady Alice was saying. "No harm will come to it."

Her castle – that's all she cares about, thought William.

"Are you sure? I promised my husband I would look after it for him."

"The duke's regent will make sure Vaudreuil Castle is undamaged," answered Lady Alice soothingly. "It will be his way of thanking you for your help and support. Now can we rely on you?"

"Of course, my Lady."

"Good. That's all I wanted to know."

William had heard enough. He slipped out of the minstrels' gallery as quietly as he could. He'd assumed Lady Alice must be plotting for her own ends when in fact she was ensuring Lady Gunnor stayed loyal to him. That was why she'd journeyed from Rouen, using Prince Edward's trip as cover. She'd simply been concerned for him and the safety of her son, Guy. He'd misjudged her terribly, and he felt awful about it.

Vaudreuil – April 1041

THE weather was cold but bright. Lucky Guy was out hunting while William was stuck inside, bored and gazing out of a window.

"They're new, aren't they?" he asked, pointing to a line of young men dressed in the brown sackcloth of monks, scurrying across the courtyard.

Constance stopped spreading clean straw on the floor, came to the window and peered out. Over the months since she'd shown William the way to the minstrels' gallery they'd become more friendly. She was a cheerful girl who, if prodded, always had gossip to pass on – the cook had been found blind drunk in the bailey or a guard had been caught with a serving girl. Her stories enlivened William's dreary days.

"They must be the novices who arrived last night, your Grace," said Constance. "The last lot left a week ago."

One wing of the castle was a seminary for monks. It was out of bounds to everyone else and the monks kept themselves to themselves. Were it not for the endless bells, calling them to chapel for the prayers that punctuated their day, William would hardly have known they were on the island.

The next morning, Constance entered William's rooms, put the breakfast tray on the bed and then paused expectantly, her cheeks flushed with excitement.

"What is it?" asked William, certain she'd discovered yet another scandal.

"I don't know if you've been told, your Grace, but one of the novices is an aristocrat. I heard Cook say he's called Lord Nicholas of Fecamp and he's the son of Duke Richard the Third. He must be a relative of yours."

"Really?" said William, sitting up excitedly. "Are you sure?"

"Quite sure, your Grace."

"Then it must be my cousin," said William, thinking back to that evening long ago in Falaise, when the studious-looking Nicholas had wished him luck. "I wonder what he's doing at Vaudreuil?"

"Cook said this new group has come from Evreux monastery. It's about a day's walk from here. They're to finish their studies under our abbot and then return, your Grace."

"I'll have to greet him," said William.

"Oh, I don't think you'll be able to," said Constance, looking shocked. "The abbot keeps them separate from the rest of us, your Grace. He's ever so strict about it..."

The sound of hurried footsteps stopped Constance

from saying more. Lady Gunnor burst into the room with Osbern behind her.

"Your Grace, a messenger has just arrived from Vimoutiers. The siege has failed! Cotentin's won!"

"How?" William was confused. The last he'd heard the siege was almost over.

"We don't know," said Osbern, as worried as Lady Gunnor.

"What about Gilbert? Is he still alive?" asked William.

"Yes, thank God. He'll come as soon as he can," said Osbern, "but with him will come trouble."

"What do you mean?" asked Lady Gunnor sharply.

"There's bound to be more fighting over the duke."

"Here, at Vaudreuil?"

"Wherever the duke is," said Osbern.

"Then perhaps he would be safer elsewhere."

"Think, Lady Gunnor," said Osbern, gently pulling her towards the door. "There is nowhere else. Now we must go and speak to the guards. They must defend William until Gilbert reaches us."

Lady Gunnor only wants me away from Vaudreuil to protect her precious castle, thought William angrily as the door shut behind them. But maybe there was sense in what she'd said. Vaudreuil looked impregnable but if Cotentin camped on the riverbanks, nobody could come or go without being seen, and eventually they'd be starved into submission. There must be somewhere better to hide. Suddenly he had an idea – but he would need help.

He looked at Constance fidgeting nervously with the breakfast she'd brought. Would she do? He studied her thoughtfully. She seemed straightforward and had helped him before. *And in any event*, he comforted himself, *she'll only know part of what I'm up to.* So he plunged in.

"About my cousin Nicholas," said William. "Could you take me to him?"

Constance stared, her eyes wide with concern.

"Your Grace, it's strictly against the abbot's and Lady Gunnor's rules."

"I know that, but I have to see him. You once told me nobody knew this castle better than you. Does that include the monastery?"

"I clean the monks' cells when they're at church, your Grace," Constance conceded.

"Could you find Nicholas's room?" asked William.

"I suppose so."

"And could you take me there?" asked William. "It's important. I wouldn't ask you if it wasn't."

There was a long pause.

"All right," said Constance at last, looking distinctly uncomfortable, "but I have to warn you, your Grace, if we get caught, it'll mean trouble."

THE very next afternoon, Constance came hurrying across the bailey to where William and Guy were shooting arrows at a target.

"May I speak with you, your Grace?"

"Ah, Rabbit is back with more important gossip," said Guy sarcastically as William moved away. He professed to hate Constance's endless chatter, saying William should be above servants' tittle-tattle, particularly from a maid who looked like a rodent.

When they were out of earshot, William said, "Ignore Guy. What is it?"

"The novices spend the morning in church, your Grace," answered Constance in almost a whisper. "Then they have lunch and are called to Nones, and after that they're alone in their cells until the abbot makes his rounds some time before the bells ring for Vespers. That's the only time I could take you to Lord Nicholas."

William was familiar with the bells which ruled the monks' days. They started at dawn, ringing for Lauds prayers. This was followed by Prime at breakfast, Terce mid-morning, Sext at noon, Nones in the afternoon, Vespers in the evening, Compline last thing at night and finally

Matins in the early hours of the morning when most of the castle slept.

"Good," said William. "You've done well. I'll see you in the hall when the bells ring for Nones, then."

"Will you be bringing Guy, your Grace? I hope you don't mind me saying, but the more there are of us, the harder it will be not to be seen."

"Don't worry. I'll be alone."

William had already decided that this was something he must do by himself. That way, if he got caught, he'd take the punishment. There was no reason for Guy to do the same, and in any event he knew how his cousin felt about Constance. He would be appalled if he knew William was so friendly with a lowly maid, and William didn't want the inevitable teasing.

Just as the chapel bells began to clang, William slipped through a small door in the Great Hall. Constance was waiting for him. He hadn't been this way before but he knew it led to the castle kitchen as servants, emerged from here at every mealtime, carrying plates of roast ox, jugs of beer and mounds of bread.

At the bottom of some steep stairs was a shaded courtyard.

"I hope no one sees us, your Grace," said Constance nervously. "I don't know what we'd say we were doing. Wait here. I'll check to see if anyone's around."

She disappeared, returning moments later looking

tense but also relieved.

"Just as I thought; no one's about. The cooks have gone for a rest and the scullery boys have disappeared. Come on."

Together they crossed the gloomy courtyard into a separate building located next to the inner battlements. It was a large, cluttered kitchen, one wall lined with shelves of pewter tankards, plates, jars and pots, and another with great iron hooks holding rabbits, brightly coloured pheasants, hams and two pig carcasses cut from snout to tail. In the hearth a cauldron was bubbling away, seething lamb. The stench of boiling meat and fat was overwhelming.

Constance hurried to a door next to the fireplace. It was bolted at both the top and the bottom.

"This leads to the monks' quarters, your Grace," she whispered. "It's the only way in from the keep. The abbot insists we go around the walls and through the main doors, but he sometimes uses it to save time."

William crouched down and pulled at the bottom lock, working it up and down as it was stiff. It gradually loosened and then jerked open. He lost his balance and fell against the wall.

"Ow, that's hot," he said, jumping up and patting his singed tunic.

"Yes, watch out!" said Constance. "That's the oven."

William touched the wall more gingerly this time. The stones were radiating heat.

"It'll be after midnight before it's cool enough to clear the ash," said Constance, tugging at the top bolt.

With a sudden yank it gave way and they were standing on the threshold of the forbidden monastery.

"Is this the time you clean?" asked William.

"No, of course not, your Grace. I only go in when they're at a service. The monks are never allowed to see women. I'd be dismissed immediately if I were seen."

Suddenly William felt awful about what he was asking her to do. If he were caught he would receive a terrible telling off from Lady Gunnor, but if Constance were caught she'd lose her job and with it a roof over her head. It was too much to risk.

"Constance, you've done enough," said William. "Tell me the way from here. I can manage."

"I wish you could, your Grace," she answered wistfully, "but it's a rabbit warren in there. You'd never find the right cell. Come on."

In silence William followed Constance along a maze of corridors lit only by saucers of fat with tiny wicks placed on the flagstone floor. Along the passageway there were countless arched doors, all firmly shut, and from behind them came the sound of mumbled chants. Carefully William memorized the way until at last Constance stopped and pointed at a door, indistinguishable from all the rest.

"That's the one," she mouthed.

"Are you sure?" he whispered.

"Certain, your Grace. It's the fourteenth door along. I checked this morning."

"Good. Go now!"

Constance shook her head firmly. "No, your Grace. You'll need me to get back. But please be quick."

Without knocking, William quietly opened the door and found himself in a cell hardly wider than his outstretched arms, with a lone crucifix on cold bare walls. At the far end was a single high window, not much more than a narrow slit, which did little to light the dreary room, and on the stone floor was a lumpy straw mattress and a small candle. Apart from this the room was empty, except for a boy of around fifteen who was kneeling on the floor absorbed in prayer, his back to William.

"Nicholas," William whispered, scared of disturbing the other novices.

The boy sprang to his feet, his pale face terrified. He had the same dark, darting eyes William remembered.

"Who are you? What are you doing here?"

"Be quiet!" urged William, desperate to stop him from crying out. "Don't you know me? I'm William, Duke of Normandy – your cousin."

Nicholas studied William's face intently.

"Is it really you?" he said at last.

"Yes. I'm staying at the castle. Gilbert sent me here because of all the troubles."

Nicholas looked shocked. "I had no idea. I only arrived last night."

"I know, but listen, I don't have much time and I need a favour. You're training to be a monk so you must be able to read and write. Would you write a letter for me?"

"Why don't you ask the abbot?" said Nicholas, looking baffled.

"It has to be secret. The duchy's in chaos. I need to ask my mother for help."

Nicholas pursed his lips and shook his head.

"I'm sorry but I can't, your Grace. Before your father left for Jerusalem he made me swear I'd never involve myself in politics but would dedicate my life to the church. Lady Alice acted as witness."

"But you also promised to serve me," William pointed out. "And all I want you to do is write a letter telling my mother that I'm at Vaudreuil."

"But I promised, your Grace."

"What my father meant was that you should never try and take my place. Think about it, Nicholas, he would have wanted you to help me. I'm your duke."

There was a long silence and William was relieved when Nicholas finally replied, "I'll write it, but how can I get it to you? We're never allowed out."

William had already thought of this.

"Just leave it under your mattress. A maid cleans these rooms when you're at Vespers. She'll check each time she comes."

There was an urgent knock at the door and Constance poked her head round anxiously.

"It's not long until the abbot does his rounds."

"What's a girl doing here?" Nicholas looked horrified.

"Don't worry, we're leaving," said William hurriedly. "Now, Nicholas, is there anything else you need?"

"Yes." He held out a heavy silver cross, around three inches long, that was dangling from a chain round his neck. "Your Grace, swear on this you won't tell anyone in the family. I don't want there to be any misunderstandings – particularly with Lady Alice."

"I swear," said William solemnly, wrapping his fingers round the cross. "And don't worry. Nothing's going to happen."

SEVERAL days later, Constance came bustling into William's room. From a fold in her shabby skirt she pulled a rolled-up piece of parchment.

"Here it is, your Grace, but please don't ask me to go again – the cook's already suspicious. Most of the girls hate cleaning those creepy cells, and I keep volunteering. I've been four times since Saturday."

"I won't, I promise," said William. "Thank you so much."

Now that he had the letter, the next question was how to get it delivered to his mother's town of Roche? The most obvious candidate, Guy, was ruled out because of his promise to Nicholas. He couldn't ask Lady Gunnor – she would never authorize anything without specific instructions from Rouen, and in any event she'd taken to her bed since the news of the fall of Vimoutiers Castle. Osbern was a possibility, but he'd always agreed with Gilbert that contact with Herleve would be the worst possible thing for William. No, his best hope was to persuade Gilbert to change his mind. The only problem was that William had no idea when Gilbert would next arrive.

"Have you still got that letter, your Grace?" said Constance a few days later when she brought a breakfast tray to William's room.

"Yes," he admitted.

"I could help."

"How? You never leave the island."

In the six months he'd been at Vaudreuil, William had seen Constance working from dawn to dusk every day of the week, cleaning, washing, and serving food. Her only rest was snatched conversations and daily prayers in the chapel.

"Your Grace, it's the festival of Mi-Carême next week and it's traditional for the younger servants to be allowed home for a couple of days. When I'm there, I could ask my brother, Ralph, to deliver the letter to Roche. He's trustworthy. I promise he wouldn't say a thing."

"Do you think you could also bring the reply back to Vaudreuil?" asked William, excitedly.

"I doubt it, your Grace. I'll only have two days at home. It won't give Ralph enough time to get there and back."

"No," said William pensively. "But Mother will find a way to deliver a reply," he continued, thinking out loud. "Are you sure he'll do it?"

"Of course, your Grace, or I wouldn't have offered. Where exactly does it have to go?"

William gave her directions to his mother's house and a small leather pouch with three gold coins in it which she immediately handed back.

"I'm not taking that, your Grace," she said.

"I didn't mean to offend you," said William. "But perhaps your family..."

Constance shook her head.

"I know, your Grace, but I daren't. If I'm caught with gold coins, I'll be hanged for stealing. I can't risk it. Besides, I'm doing this because I want to."

* * *

The weather was still bitter, but neither William nor Guy could face another day playing cards by the fire, trying not to dwell on what was happening beyond the water. Rumours abounded: Cotentin was gathering an army and would soon be heading for Vaudreuil; Gacé, determined not to be outdone by his rival, was assembling his own men, and somewhere in the mix must be Gilbert, battling on William's behalf.

Whatever the outcome, for good or evil, William knew one of them would arrive and claim him. It was wearing and eerie, waiting on this isolated island week after week, not knowing who was coming for him – but what choice did he have?

To try and distract the listless boys, Osbern arranged for a straw target to be set up in the courtyard.

"What's that?" asked Guy as he lifted a first arrow to his bow. He pulled the string taut and it flew through the air and thumped into the bull's-eye.

"What?" asked William.

Guy pointed to a tiny white triangle of parchment protruding from the pocket of William's cloak. A letter! At once William smiled. It must be the reply he'd been waiting for. His mother had found a way.

"Something from the abbot," he said, concealing his excitement, "probably a prayer."

Guy looked sceptical. "Really? I didn't know he sent you those."

William shrugged. "Only sometimes."

Target practice crawled by. All William wanted to do was have the letter read to him, but it would look suspicious if he stopped shooting before his quiver was empty. At last, when they had each shot twenty arrows, William returned to his rooms.

"See you at supper," he said as he walked away.

As soon as he'd shut his door he unfolded the paper. It was covered with cramped, spidery and, to William, indecipherable, writing. He must go straight to Nicholas.

Within the hour William had found his way to what he thought was his cousin's door. He wished Constance was there to reassure him he had the right one. All the doors along the gloomy passageway were identical. Could he possibly have got it wrong?

Stop worrying, he told himself, and plunged inside. To his relief, Nicholas turned towards him in surprise.

"What are you doing here, your Grace?" his cousin whispered anxiously.

William held out the parchment.

"It's the reply. Please read it."

"But the abbot will soon be here." Nicholas's dark eyes darted to the door as if he expected it to be opened at any moment.

"I thought he didn't come in the afternoons," said William. "That's what Constance told me."

"Except during Lent, your Grace. You'll have to come back tomorrow."

Nicholas was now biting his lip in anxiety, but William couldn't wait; he'd wasted too much time already.

"Please," he pleaded. "It won't take long."

He unfolded the letter and held it up for Nicholas to see.

With a nervous sigh, his cousin took the precious note and read haltingly,

> "'Dear son, I was so happy to receive your
> letter after all this time and to know that you
> are safe. However, I must warn you that your
> situation is becoming more perilous each day.
> Help is on the way. I'm sending a friend.
> He'll be at the church in the village of Pîtres,
> close to Vaudreuil at midday on St Stephen's
> Day. You must meet him there.
> Your loving mother.'"

"How many days is it until then?" William asked impatiently.

"Let me work it out," said Nicholas, counting on his

fingers. "Five."

Five days! It was no time to make a plan to get off the island and get to Pîtres, over a mile away.

A church bell began to toll.

"The abbot will be starting his rounds," said Nicholas, pale and anxious. "You must go!"

Quickly William pulled open the cell door and then stopped. He could hear footsteps coming up the stairs and the heavy wheezing of the stout abbot. He leapt back into the cell.

"Is there nowhere for me to hide?" asked William.

Nicholas shook his head. "I'm afraid not," he said, as the footsteps got closer and closer.

15

"CAN I get out if I go along the corridor?" asked William.

"No."

"Then I'll creep by when the abbot goes into the cell next door."

"You can't," said Nicholas hopelessly. "Brother Hugh always waits outside in the corridor."

There must be somewhere to hide, thought William, looking frantically round the narrow room, but apart from the thin mattress it was empty. *Well, at least I can keep the contents of the letter secret*, he decided quickly, snatching the parchment from the astonished Nicholas and putting a corner of it into the candle's flame. The paper curled up, blackened and turned to cinders. William only just had time to stamp on the crimson ashes before the cell door was pushed open.

A man stood in the doorway. His black, hooded habit hid much of his face, but there was no mistaking his fury.

"Novices are not allowed to fraternize when they should be at prayer. You know that!" he bellowed at Nicholas.

"S-sorry, sir."

Nicholas was quaking too much to speak clearly, but now that William had destroyed the letter, he felt calmer.

"Who are you and what are you doing here?" said the abbot, turning his rage on William.

"I am William, Duke of Normandy," answered William grandly, "and I am here on a family matter – visiting my cousin."

The abbot was taken aback, caught between surprise and indignation.

"Your Grace," he blustered, "I didn't recognize you. But nobody outside the order may see a novice, not even the duke. They're at a very delicate stage in their instruction."

"Yes, Nicholas was just explaining that to me," said William trying to look contrite. "I must apologize and I want you to know that it wasn't Nicholas who broke the rules. It was my fault. You do understand that, don't you? I would not want him to be punished for my mistake."

"Of course, your Grace," said the abbot through gritted teeth. "But I must ask you to leave immediately. Brother Hugh will show you out and I'm afraid I will have to take the matter up with Lady Gunnor."

"You may do as you wish," said William, praying he'd done enough to spare his cousin any punishment.

He followed Brother Hugh through the monastery and out of its front gate on the far side of the island. They walked along a long narrow path that hugged the castle walls, past the cesspit and then back through the main portcullis and into the first bailey. The abbot, however, must have used the short cut through the kitchen, for when William reached the Great Hall, Lady Gunnor was waiting for him. She was sitting on a stool by the fire, her back ramrod-straight. William hadn't seen her since she'd retreated to her bed after the fall of Vimoutiers and the change in her was striking. Normally Lady Gunnor was an elegant and fastidious dresser, but now her wine-coloured gown hung loosely and her face was drawn and pale.

She wasted no time on pleasantries. "Your Grace, I'm very disappointed in you. I told you exactly where you could and could not go in this castle and you have deliberately disobeyed me. The abbot is most upset. Things are bad enough without this."

"I only wanted to see my cousin," said William, trying the same excuse on Lady Gunnor. "I didn't think there could be much harm in that."

"Well, you should have come to me first. For your information, Nicholas won't be on the island much longer, so there will be no chance of you seeing him again."

"What do you mean?" asked William.

"The abbot has decided to move him back to Evreux where he can complete his studies without being disturbed. Now I must insist that you do not misbehave like this again."

If only that were possible, thought William, but it wasn't. One way or another he was going to have to get off the island in only five days' time and to do that he would have to break all Lady Gunnor's rules.

16

WILLIAM spent much of the next four days trying to work out if there was a way to get off Vaudreuil without being seen. Guards stood at the gates of the inner and outer battlements and would never let him past without telling Lady Gunnor. Then there was that vast, fast-moving, choppy river. Its water was freezing and it was too wide to swim across. He would need a boat and there wasn't always one moored at the jetty. It was hopeless. Saint Stephen's Day was tomorrow and he still didn't have a plan. Not for the first time, he felt trapped on the wretched island.

Rain lashed against the shutters and the room was chilly despite the fire that burned in the hearth. William was warming his hands and, for what felt like the thousandth time, trying to work out how to get to Pîtres when a messenger arrived from Lady Gunnor: he must come to the Great Hall immediately. Gilbert had arrived.

William's prayers had been answered. Here was the one man who could tell Lady Gunnor to let him leave.

He found Gilbert in the Great Hall, his boots splattered with mud, his beautiful azure tunic ripped and his left hand bandaged with a dirty cloth. He was sweating profusely and trying to catch his breath. Osbern and Lady Gunnor were with him.

"Your Grace, I came as soon as I could," he said. "We were defeated. Cotentin and Gacé are racing here. There was nothing I could do to stop them."

"They're coming to Vaudreuil?" said Lady Gunnor, aghast. "Why?"

"For William. Whoever controls him controls the duchy, and neither wants the other to win."

"Oh Lord, what should we do?" asked Lady Gunnor.

"We must make peace with one of them," said Gilbert. "I don't have enough men to defend William for long, not even on Vaudreuil."

"Not enough men!" said William. "Has everyone deserted me?"

"Not everyone, your Grace, but many. They're afraid of being punished by whoever wins."

Lady Gunnor jumped to her feet and began pacing frantically in front of the fire. "The duke must leave. He should not be here," she said.

"I've told you before, saying that won't save your skin or your precious home," said Osbern bitterly. "You'll only be punished if he leaves the castle."

"I'm not thinking of myself," said Lady Gunnor. "I'm thinking of the hundreds of people that live here, some of them monks doing God's work. If the castle cannot be defended, why should it be destroyed? It would be safer for the duke to leave while he still can."

"Only if we can think of somewhere else to shelter him, and I can't," said Osbern, "and neither can you."

He turned to Gilbert. "If it's hopeless and we must surrender, who do you advise William should surrender to?"

"Gacé. He's ruthless but once he has what he wants he's fair, and he might be persuaded to rule as regent, leaving William as Duke. Cotentin, on the other hand, is an animal and a devious one at that. He's rumoured to have another duke in mind, someone else from the family. Perhaps Richard's boy."

William was certain that wasn't right. Nicholas would have warned him. And what was all this talk of surrender? He was a knight, not a coward. He suddenly thought of his father. It was impossible to imagine Robert cravenly yielding to one of his nobles, particularly one who'd taken an oath of allegiance to him, and he wasn't going to either.

"Since my family invaded Normandy, we've never surrendered to anyone," he said firmly.

"If I thought fighting would make any difference I would be the first to recommend it, your Grace," said Gilbert wearily. "But we're hopelessly outnumbered. This way Gacé might be persuaded to protect you."

"Only until I'm old enough to rule myself and then he'll want me out of the way," said William.

"I'm not so sure. If Gacé's beaten Cotentin, that may be enough, your Grace. I don't like it any more than you do, but my biggest worry at the moment is that Cotentin will get here first. The most my men and I can do is try and delay him so Gacé has a chance."

"May I have a private word with you?" said William.

As soon as they were alone he said, "Gilbert, would you be giving me the same advice if I had somewhere to go to?"

"I'm not sure, your Grace. Why?"

"Tomorrow I'm meeting someone in the graveyard of Pîtres church. I'm not sure who, but they've been sent by my mother."

"By Herleve?"

"Yes. When I heard about the situation at Vimoutiers I managed to get a message to her. She wrote to tell me help arrives tomorrow."

Gilbert was silent for a moment.

"Who have you told about this?"

"The only person who knows is my cousin Nicholas."

"Nicholas could be working for Cotentin."

"He isn't," said William firmly.

"How can you be so sure, your Grace?"

"I just am. Believe me."

Gilbert shrugged his shoulders. "And you say the meeting is tomorrow?"

"Yes, at midday. I want you to help me get there."

"No," said Gilbert resolutely. "It might be a trap."

"But I must," protested William.

"Your Grace, I'll go instead and check that it's safe.

Meanwhile don't tell a soul. Tomorrow night we'll decide what to do but until then stay in your room. There's nowhere else that's secure."

17

VAUDREUIL – MAY 1041

EARLY the next morning William watched from his window as Gilbert left the island. He was dressed in a long maroon cloak, chainmail and the same tatty blue tunic he'd worn the night before. Gilbert must have felt William's gaze on him for, as he jumped into the bobbing ferry, he scanned the castle, identified William's window and raised his hand in salute.

Just then William heard a sound and turned to find Guy opening the door.

"Oh, you're here," he said, looking surprised. He was wearing a grey hooded cloak that trailed along the ground.

"Of course I'm here," replied William. "I'm hardly allowed anywhere else. Are you going out or do you want to play a game of chess?"

Guy took off the cloak. "No, I'll play," he said, but with little enthusiasm.

"What's up?" asked William, as he easily checkmated Guy. Usually his cousin was incredibly competitive, planning complicated moves, determined to beat William, but this morning something was distracting him. "Is there anything wrong?"

"No, nothing," answered Guy sullenly.

They played another game, but neither of them had their hearts in it. It was the first beautiful day of spring and they were stuck inside and all the while William couldn't help wondering what Gilbert had discovered. It was so frustrating not being able to tell Guy what was on his mind.

The chapel bells rang for Terce.

"Don't you want to go out today?" asked Guy.

"Of course I do, but you know the orders."

Guy looked at him steadily. "I could distract Martin, then you could go for a wander."

William was tempted. The time would pass much more quickly until Gilbert returned with news.

"What about you?"

"I can go when I like. It's you that's stuck," said Guy.

"All right, but how will you do it?" asked William, intrigued.

"I'll call Martin to my room. Then you can sneak past, but make sure you close your door behind you, then he'll think you're still inside." He threw over the old grey cloak. "Put this on, and no one will realize it's you."

The hood fell over William's forehead, casting a shadow, and hiding every lock of his distinctive red hair.

"As long as you don't get too close to anyone, you'll be fine," reassured Guy.

Minutes later William was down the stairs and out in the bailey. Despite the bright sun, the morning was crisp with a chilly easterly wind – just the weather for wrapping up warm. He took care to cover his face and discovered Guy was right – in the courtyard people were far too busy gossiping, cleaning out the pigsty and carrying water from the well to notice him.

It was a relief to move around freely without servants respectfully stopping what they were doing and bobbing a curtsey or a bow whenever he got close. Since that fateful evening when his father had named him his heir, William, the Duke, had become an object of curiosity – but not this morning. Wondering how far he could get, he crossed the bailey to the first gate, and was surprised to find there were no guards. The two large wooden doors were closed – latched but not locked. William unfastened one and slipped through, pushing the doors together once more. He was standing between two stone walls, in the grassy space between the two sets of fortifications. Guy and William often came there for archery practice as there was no danger of anyone getting hit by a stray arrow.

William wandered aimlessly round until he reached the portcullis, the main entrance to the castle, and discovered that here again there were no guards. The castle steward must have called a meeting but it seemed strange that not even a couple of men had been left to keep watch. He slipped through this final gate. At the bottom of the craggy jetty was an empty rowing boat, moored with a single rope, bobbing round in the breeze. William couldn't believe it; all this time he'd been worrying about how to get off Vaudreuil without being seen, and it was this simple! Pîtres was only a mile away. If only he'd left earlier, he could have walked there and met whoever it was and nobody would have noticed.

He went back through the courtyard and into the bailey and was just heading towards the keep when a whole jumble of people came pouring out, Constance among them. She was wearing her usual brown skirt and a pale shirt and her long hair was piled in a disorganized bun. In each hand she held a bucket. William followed her to the well and, when he was sure he was out of anyone else's hearing, called to her.

She looked at him, perplexed, looked again, realized who it was under the shadowy hood and smiled her toothy grin.

"Your Grace, you should be in your room," she admonished gently. "You're not trying to get into the monastery again, are you?"

"No, don't worry. I just felt like getting out. But where is everybody?"

"Lady Gunnor called a meeting. She insisted absolutely everyone come. All except you, Vicomte Guy and Martin, I think."

"Why? What was it about?"

"Instructions on what to do if the castle is attacked, your Grace. How everybody should keep to their posts, that sort of thing."

So Lady Gunnor must think an attack was imminent. He'd better get back to his room before she checked up on him.

As he opened the door to his bedchamber, Guy jumped.

"I thought you'd be longer," he said hastily and they went back to playing their listless game of chess. As the light began to fade Constance arrived with a tray of beer, some bread and a leg of ham.

"You must have something for us, Rabbit," said Guy. "What petty gossip is there from the kitchens to enliven our day?"

"None, sir."

"Really?" said William.

The way she was sucking her bottom lip told him that wasn't the truth; something had happened.

"Nothing that Vicomte Guy would be interested in, your Grace," said Constance, a little tetchily.

"Well, *I'm* interested," said William.

"Yes, come on, Rabbit. His Grace is always interested in the little people's affairs."

"Shut up, Guy," said William. "What's going on?"

"There's been trouble in the village," said Constance, directing her words at William as she arranged the food on a cloth on the chest.

"Which village?"

"Pîtres, your Grace. A knight's been killed – ambushed in the churchyard. A boy found him there when he went to fetch the priest."

"Rabbit has finally unearthed something of interest," said Guy. "It must be one of Cotentin's men. They're closer than we thought."

But William was not thinking of Cotentin's men.

"Did you hear the name of the man that was killed?" he asked Constance, dreading the reply.

"No, your Grace, but Lady Gunnor insisted that the body be brought back to the castle. The ferryman's just brought it across. I heard about it when the cook came running in saying he's covered in blood and his throat's been slit from here to here!" She dramatically traced her finger from one ear to the other. "He's been laid in the chapel."

William was on his feet.

"You can't leave again!" said Guy.

But William didn't care. He ran, two steps at a time, down the winding staircase and across the muddy bailey to the small chapel. The church was lit by flickering candles. Ahead of him he saw the green linen of Lady Gunnor's dress and Osbern's brown tunic. They were standing in the nave with their backs to him.

William crept forward as silently as he could. He didn't want to be seen until he knew for certain who was lying on the altar. He could see two limp feet, shod in muddy leather boots with a knight's spurs attached. Then a cape – deep azure, the very same colour that had caught his attention that morning.

"It's Gilbert, isn't it?" he said.

Lady Gunnor spun round, her eyes puffy and swollen. She wiped them hastily.

"Your Grace, you should not be here," she said. "Steward Osbern, please take the duke back to his room."

"Madam, you forget he was my guardian. I must pay my respects," said William.

He climbed the last two steps to the altar. There lay Gilbert, his face unnaturally pale and his eyes closed. His blue tunic was stained brownish-red and someone had tied a scarf round his neck to hide his hideous injury.

"Who did this?" whispered William.

"We don't know," Osbern replied. "For some reason he stopped at the church and that's where he was ambushed. It's hard to understand why but we think they must have been waiting for someone else."

And William knew who. Somehow, his secret correspondence with his mother had been betrayed, but how? He suddenly realized that he had no idea who'd put his mother's reply in his coat pocket that day at target practice. He ran through the possible list – Nicholas, Constance, and her brother, Ralph, were the only people who knew about the letter. One of them must have betrayed him, but who? Nicholas? For some reason he couldn't believe that. Ralph? But surely he would do what his sister told him... It must be Constance. Constance who seemed so innocent but who knew so much. She must be the traitor! She'd put his mother's letter in his cloak and before she did so she'd allowed his enemies to read it. It made William furious to realize how stupid he'd been. He should never have trusted someone he knew so little. And yet she'd always seemed so honest. She was one of the few people who had made his time at Vaudreuil bearable and to think that it was all a pretence! But why? Was it for money? He would find out, and then she must pay for Gilbert's murder.

18

"WHAT happened?" asked Guy when William returned to his rooms escorted by Osbern and Lady Gunnor.

"Gilbert's been killed. He was assassinated this afternoon."

"The duke's enemies are getting closer – William's life could be in danger," said Lady Gunnor. "I've ordered extra guards. There'll be two on each floor of the North Tower and two at the entrance in the Great Hall."

"Who have you put on?" asked William.

"Along with Martin, your Grace, I'll add Jacques, Matthew, Ben and Luc."

William pictured the four men. They were brawny, tough lads from the local farms who had lived and worked on Lady Gunnor's lands their entire lives. Nobody would get past them.

"Guy," said Osbern, 'it's getting late. Go downstairs." He waited until everyone had left and then added, "I'll be sleeping here from now on. There's room for two."

"Are you sure that's necessary?" asked William.

"Yes. I'd never forgive myself if anything happened to you."

William knew Osbern was not going to change his

mind so he climbed into bed, pulled the curtains and blew out the only candle.

The room was pitch-black. Soon the only sounds were the north wind whistling round the turret and Osbern's steady snores, but William found he couldn't sleep. The sight of Gilbert lying stricken on that altar haunted him. It was his fault Gilbert was dead and he shuddered knowing that same dreadful fate would have befallen him if he had gone in his place.

He heard the night watchman call midnight and then it seemed no time at all before the bells rang for Matins. William had been tossing and turning, snatching only minutes of unhappy sleep, for hours. Now all was quiet, even the wind had dropped. His throat was dry. Perhaps it would help to drink something.

He drew back the curtain and slipped out of bed, careful not to disturb Osbern. It was still dark but he knew his room well enough to walk over to the chest where Constance left a fresh jug of water each night. As he picked up the jug he heard something – it sounded like muffled footsteps outside – and froze, waiting for Martin and the new guards to challenge whoever it was that was creeping round. Nothing happened. The footsteps were getting closer and closer. William's heart was racing. Who could possibly be outside his room at this time at night and what did they want with him?

As the door creaked open, William slipped behind the heavy drape that curtained off the privy and listened intently. There were several indistinguishable bumps and then the noise of feet padding round. It sounded like a couple of people, one of whom dragged his foot across the wooden floor.

William stayed as still as he could, not daring to make a sound. At any moment he expected the curtain to be ripped open and to be hauled out. Suddenly he remembered Osbern – his snoring had stopped but why hadn't he made a noise? Just then there was a thud and a stifled sigh. William was desperate to know what was happening on the other side of the curtain. A hundred questions raced through his mind. What had happened to his guards? And how long before the intruders discovered him?

"Are you sure you've done it?" came a hoarse whisper.

"He won't wake up, don't worry," said another man, with an ugly chuckle. "Let's go."

William was so petrified he didn't move. Only when several minutes had passed did he creep out, go to the window ledge and feel for a flint. His hands were shaking so much that he had to strike it three times before he could light the lamp. He held up the quivering flame and looked around, but the room was bare. Where was Osbern? Quickly he pulled back the bed drapes. Osbern was lying absolutely still with a pillow over his head. William leant down and listened to his chest. He could hear nothing. No breath, no heartbeat, just a terrible silence. Slowly, he lifted a corner of the pillow and Osbern's lifeless eyes stared up at him, his neck bruised purple and blue. He'd been suffocated. In the dark, the intruders had made a mistake and murdered him instead of William.

The young duke had never felt so scared or alone. The two people closest to him – Gilbert and Osbern – had been murdered. Whoever had ordered these attacks would come back for him. Vaudreuil was no longer a refuge but a trap, and a trap he must escape. He must find Guy, his only friend in this godforsaken place, and together they must flee.

He pulled open the chest and dressed quickly in a cloak, tunic, britches and leather boots, but as he hurried to the door he heard a sound that sent shivers down his spine – more footsteps echoing up the turret.

19

WILLIAM blew out the lamp, grabbed his dagger and stood behind the door.

"Your Grace! Are you all right?"

He should've known it wouldn't be long before Constance turned up.

Unsure whether she was alone, William stood in wait, still as a statue behind the wooden door, ready to strike. He might not get out of the tower alive, but he would not be taken without a fight.

"Your Grace?" Constance's voice trembled with alarm.

William didn't answer.

"Are you there?"

He peered through the gap between the door and its frame. There she was, alone, in a grey linen nightdress with a white nightcap and a candle in her hand. Her wiry hair was unbrushed but she didn't look sleepy. Her eyes were wide and apprehensive and her large front teeth were anxiously biting her bottom lip. Biding his time, William waited until she crossed the threshold, then grabbed her by the back of the neck and held a dagger to her throat.

"What are you doing?" she cried out, terrified.

"You're the one who should be answering that," said

William. "Who are you working for?"

"I don't know what you're talking about," said Constance.

"What, none of it?" said William sarcastically. "Not the letter, not Gilbert's death, not tonight?"

"No, your Grace," Constance whimpered. "P-please don't kill me. I only came to see if you were all right."

"In the middle of the night?"

"I couldn't sleep, knowing that gentleman was laying stone-cold dead in the chapel. I kept tossing and turning, driving the other maids mad, so I got up. That's when I noticed there were no guards at the bottom of your stairs. I thought it was strange, as I knew Lady Gunnor had ordered them, and then I had an awful feeling that something was wrong. Halfway up the stairs I found Martin, stabbed in the chest, and I feared the worst for you. Honestly, that's all."

William looked at the trembling girl, pleading for her life. She would say anything to save her skin.

"What about the letter? Are you telling me you didn't tell anyone about that?"

"I swear I didn't, your Grace," said Constance. "I'll swear on the cross, if you'll let me."

This made William pause. Lying on the holy cross was a sin. Would she really risk her soul? Could it be Nicholas after all? *No*, he thought, *guilty people say anything when they're trapped.* He mustn't let Constance persuade him with her tricks and he had to know who she was working for.

"Who paid you to do this?" he asked.

"I swear, nobody has paid me for anything, your Grace," said Constance. She was speaking quickly, knowing her life depended on it. "When I was up, I looked out of the window and a light caught my eye. It was Vicomte Guy in the bailey. I was about to run and tell him about the missing guards when I noticed he was talking to two other men. Something didn't seem right. I was scared for you so I came here first."

William was getting more and more confused. Was Constance suggesting Guy was involved? Impossible. Guy was his oldest friend. They'd grown up together from the time they left for Paris all those years ago. Guy was his cousin and his closest confidant. He would never betray him. Constance didn't like him and was just trying to detract attention from her own guilt.

"You're lying to me!"

William gripped her neck even more tightly.

"I'm not, your Grace," she squealed. "I saw him creeping round the bailey with two men – one of them had a limp."

One of the intruders *had* dragged his leg, thought William, but then Constance would know that. *She's trying to trick me again.* It made him even more furious.

"I don't believe you," he said, pulling her so close the dagger blade was resting against her throat. "You're a witch spreading lies but it won't work."

"If you don't believe me, see for yourself," squeaked Constance.

"Fine," said William. "I will."

Roughly he pulled the frightened girl down the twisting staircase. Round the second bend he found Martin, the guard, slumped across the stairs.

"He's dead, your Grace," said Constance, realizing how shocked William was. "There's nothing you can do for him."

William climbed over the body, sickened at the thought of stepping on a finger or limb, and opened the door to the room that Osbern and Guy shared.

"Give me your candle."

Holding up the light, he called, "Guy, wake up! It's me!"

There was no answer. The bed was empty.

William dragged Constance to the window. The courtyard was so misty and dark she couldn't have seen a thing. Just as he'd thought, she was lying. Then, by the well, a movement caught his eye in the fog. He peered more closely. Figures *were* creeping about. As he stared he began to distinguish between them. There were two men, plus the unmistakable silhouette of short, stocky Guy and a slim, tall woman – Lady Gunnor – all huddled together conspiratorially. They must be in league; Constance *had* been telling the truth.

"Could Guy have read your mother's letter, your Grace?" asked Constance quietly.

It was possible. He or Lady Gunnor could have somehow intercepted it and decided to use the information it contained to have him killed. But why wait for that? He'd been in their power for months. Something must have changed – could it be the thought of Cotentin and Gacé rushing towards Vaudreuil? Perhaps Lady Gunnor had finally lost her nerve and decided to ingratiate herself with whoever arrived first to try and save her castle.

As William thought about it, more and more pieces of the jigsaw fell into place. The perplexed look on Guy's face when William returned from wandering round the castle yesterday and how Lady Gunnor had ordered the guards to a meeting, leaving him free to leave. They'd *wanted* him to go to Pîtres, where an assassin was waiting. In fact, they'd virtually pushed him out of the door, but they hadn't known about Gilbert. No wonder she was crying over his body – it was the wrong one!

And William suddenly realized how wrong he'd been. Guy, who was so proud of his nobility, was a traitor and Constance, the daughter of peasants, was the most loyal and brave person he'd ever met. She'd climbed over Martin's body and up to William's room to try and save him, not knowing who might be lying in wait. William wasn't sure if he'd have been that brave. As for Guy, he was a traitor and a coward, and one day he'd pay for his betrayal.

"YOUR Grace, the candle!" warned Constance.

Too late, William saw one of the figures below pointing up at the turret.

"We've got to get out of here," he said.

They flew down the stairs to the Great Hall. The floor was covered with sleeping soldiers, maids, scullery boys and minstrels resting their heads on their mandolins.

"Constance, save yourself while there's still time; nobody knows you're with me," whispered William.

"No! You'll need me if you're going to get out of here alive."

"I can manage by myself."

"Think, your Grace. How many of the people here could have taken bribes from Vicomte Guy or Lady Gunnor? Any one of them might betray you. I won't."

Just then the castle jester, sleeping only feet away from them, groaned and rolled over onto his side, the bells on his ridiculous red and blue costume jangling. The man lying next to him mumbled a complaint. William and Constance froze, not wanting to wake anyone, but knowing that at any moment Guy or Lady Gunnor might return.

Constance spoke first.

"Go that way, your Grace," she pointed at a door in the far corner of the hall. "They'll come up the eastern staircase. Come on! We don't have any time to spare!"

As quickly as they dared, they picked their way across the hall. The glowing embers in the fireplaces at either end of the room gave off enough light for them to see the outlines of the sleeping bodies. Some were snoring, others were silent. William held his breath, not wanting to disturb them from their slumber. They were halfway across the room when he caught Constance's eye and gave her an encouraging smile, but as he did so he felt something soft under his left foot – it was the cook's toe!

"Oi, what are you playing at?" said the cook sleepily, rubbing his eyes.

Constance was immediately by his side, apologizing while surreptitiously gesturing at William to get going. He stole away as quietly as he could and ran down a flight of stairs, stopping only when he was certain he was out of sight.

He waited for what felt like an age. What could Constance possibly be doing? Had she been caught? Should he leave without her? But William suddenly realized he didn't want to. Constance knew her way about the castle and would be useful to him, but it was more than that. He was all alone and he had no idea where he was going. In all of Normandy, Constance was now his only friend, so he waited in the stairwell, conscious that every second that passed could cost him dear. Finally she appeared, breathless and apologetic, with a brown skirt over her nightdress and a tatty woollen wrap round her shoulders.

"The cook asked me to get him some beer," she explained quickly as they hurried down the stairs, "so I went to the kitchen and then grabbed my shawl and skirt. I wasn't sure if you'd wait and I'm not sure you should have…"

"Why? What's wrong?" asked William.

"As I slipped through the door I saw some men coming into the hall. I think one of them was Guy and I'm certain he saw me."

21

WILLIAM and Constance ran down the stairs and out into the bailey.

"Head for the gate," said Constance breathlessly, "and pray there's a boat at the jetty."

"There's no time. Quick, in here!"

William grabbed Constance's hand and pulled her through the nearest door. They found themselves standing in the kitchen.

"We're trapped – there's nowhere to hide," said Constance.

"What about the oven?"

"Cook baked bread this evening. It'll be boiling."

Footsteps pounded towards them – their pursuers were just outside.

"It'll have to do."

As William opened the iron door the escaping heat singed his skin. The huge oven was wide enough to roast a whole ox and tall enough for Constance to stand straight, although William, at almost a foot taller, had to bend uncomfortably. He pulled the door behind them. It was sweltering. The bricks under their feet were so scorching they had to jump from foot to foot.

In the darkness William pulled off his cloak and untied his tunic. Sweat was pouring off him and each breath burnt his dry throat.

"How long must we stay here?" asked Constance, sounding panicky in the darkness. "It's so hot. I think I'm going to faint."

William felt that he too would pass out at any moment. The heat was unbearable and his back was aching from his awkward crouch.

Just then they heard voices and the sound of a pot smashing.

"Damn it!" said Guy. "I can't see a thing. Where does this door lead?"

His voice sounded so close, he must be standing right outside the oven. *Please don't look in here*, William silently prayed.

A male voice William didn't recognize answered, "It takes you to the monastery, sir, but I doubt the duke would know that."

"That's where you're wrong," said Guy triumphantly. "He's been there before. I reckon that's exactly where he'll be hiding."

There was the scraping of metal bolts and then the footsteps faded into silence. William couldn't believe his luck. The monastery was a labyrinth. Guy would be busy searching it for ages. He pushed open the oven door and stumbled out, gasping for breath. Constance tottered out behind him.

"Are you all right?" he asked as she sat down heavily on the nearest stool.

"I just need a moment, your Grace," she said, breathing in the fresh, cool air. "Could you get me some water?"

William grabbed a jug from the table and smelt it. It was beer but it would have to do – he couldn't waste precious time running to the well.

"Have this."

As she drank, William asked, "Constance, is there any way to get off Vaudreuil without being seen by the guards?"

She paused for a moment, then smiled. "You know, I think there is, your Grace," she said, pointing at a tall wicker basket with two wooden wheels at its base in the corner of the kitchen. It was the rubbish bin.

"How's that going to help?"

"It's almost dawn. I often take it out at about this time; the sentries will think nothing of it. But we must hurry."

The basket was half full of chicken bones, broken pottery and stinking, rotten vegetables. As William climbed in, he sank up to his knees in slimy waste and then had to squat for the lid to close above him. The smell was appalling, making him gag. He felt the basket tilt and Constance straining as she pulled it along. Although she was sturdy and strong, William knew it must be a struggle.

As he was bumped from side to side, he tried to keep track of where he was. He calculated they must be almost across the first bailey when Constance paused.

"You're up early," said a jolly voice.

"There's a lot to do today," said Constance. "I thought I'd make a start."

Inside the putrid basket, William held his breath. Would the guard fall for it?

"Hold on and I'll unlock the gates for you."

The doors creaked open. They were through the first wall.

The basket bounced across the second courtyard to the main portcullis.

"You've got your hands full," called a soldier as they approached the last gate.

"I know," answered Constance. "One of the kitchen boys forgot to do it yesterday."

"I'll give you a hand," said the guard.

William's heart was in his mouth.

"No, it's fine," said Constance cheerfully, but William could hear the anxiety in her voice.

"I'll close the gate after you, then. Lady Gunnor's very strict about it. Knock when you want to come back in."

The final gate creaked open and the basket bumped and jolted its way down the stairs carved into the rocks. As its contents were shaken up a piece of rotten turnip caught William on the cheek and covered his hand with slime as he wiped it away, but he didn't mind. Constance had done it. He was nearly free.

At last the basket was set straight.

"You can come out, your Grace," Constance whispered excitedly. "And look, there's a boat."

William climbed out and flicked the rancid mess from his britches as best as he could. There in the grey early morning mist a ferry was bobbing round in the water and, miraculously, there was no ferryman to be seen.

"I don't know how to thank you, Constance. I could never have done it without you," said William, and together they hurried down the last few steps towards the jetty and freedom.

22

"ARE you ready?" asked William.

"Hold on, your Grace," said Constance, putting the second oar in its rowlock. "Yes, let's go."

"Not so fast!" Guy emerged from the mist, holding a bow and arrow which he was pointing straight at William. He walked slowly down the stone steps. "One move and I'll fire."

There was no chance of him missing from this distance so William stood absolutely still. Whatever he did, he mustn't provoke Guy, but his mind was whirring, trying desperately to think of a way out.

"You won't get away this time," continued Guy, only ten feet away and not taking his fierce blue eyes off William for a moment. His aristocratic face broke into a spiteful smile as he taunted his cousin. "I told Lady Gunnor I'd watch the jetty. When my men have finished searching the monastery they'll find us here."

"And then what?" asked William bitterly.

"Then Cotentin will deal with you and I'll be duke."

Gilbert had said Cotentin had a member of the family lined up – now William knew who it was.

"How could you?" he asked. "What did I do to deserve this?"

"You stole my duchy."

"What are you talking about?" asked William incredulously.

"Duke Robert was *my* uncle. When he died it should have come to *me*."

"But I'm his son."

"You! You're nothing but a half-breed, with a peasant as his only friend." Guy spat the words out.

"At least Constance is loyal," said William.

"As my mother says, loyalty isn't everything. You must take back what's yours, if it's been stolen."

So Lady Alice *was* behind this. But what of the conversation he'd overhead in the minstrels' gallery? William remembered her promising Lady Gunnor: *The duke's regent will make sure Vaudreuil Castle is undamaged. It will be his way of thanking you for your help and support.* Then he realized – he'd made a terrible mistake. Lady Alice hadn't been talking about Gilbert, she'd been talking about Cotentin, the regent she'd arranged for her son. That was why she'd come all the way from Rouen – she needed to make sure Lady Gunnor was on her side. William should have trusted his instincts. He should have known Lady Alice would poison Guy's mind. After all, she'd like nothing better than to be mother of the Duke of Normandy.

"And when did she say that?" William asked. "Was it when she was persuading Lady Gunnor to betray me? Can't any of you make up your own mind about what's right or wrong?"

"I know what's wrong," said Guy indignantly. "It's how little respect I've been given. You didn't stop Gilbert snubbing me. You allowed King Henry to knight you and not me. You even blessed Prince Edward without me. My mother told me I shouldn't put up with it any longer."

William couldn't believe it. He knew Guy hated being in the shadow of his younger cousin, but to bear this kind of grudge was ridiculous. And yet he'd been warned all those years ago in Falaise by his mother: *Your father's side of the family is more complicated and you should be wary of them. They all have ambitions of their own ... always be on your guard.* He should have heeded her words.

"So, Lady Alice talked you into this," said William.

"No!" answered Guy fiercely. "I defended you. All the time we were in Rouen, she kept pulling me aside and pointing things out and I told her she was wrong. I said you were my friend. But when Lady Gunnor showed me the letter – the one some boy tried to bribe the ferryman to bring to you – I knew that my mother had been right all along. You were plotting without me. Even your Rabbit maid knew about it, but you told me nothing. You, a bastard, treating me like that! I swore then to take my revenge and claim what was rightfully mine."

"I didn't tell you about the letter because I couldn't," said William. "Nicholas made me promise. He was terrified of breaking an oath he'd made to your mother."

"I don't trust a word you say anymore," said Guy.

"So you've decided to trust Cotentin instead?" said William sarcastically. "The man's a snake. He'll use you to get the duchy for himself."

"That's not true. And anyway just look at you ... your protectors are dead. You've nowhere to hide. You're as good as dead."

"That's not quite true," said a gruff voice. A bearded man in his early thirties emerged from the cold mist and grabbed the startled Guy round the neck. In his confusion Guy dropped his bow which clattered down the last two steps and into the river.

"Your Grace, jump into the boat!" ordered the stranger.

Quickly William did as he was told.

"What do you want me to do with him?" asked the man, frowning down at Guy.

William looked at his cousin, locked in the stranger's arm, clawing frantically with his fingers to escape. A small part of him felt sorry for Guy but mostly he was livid. Once a traitor, always a traitor. He could show no mercy.

"Kill him!" he said coldly. "Kill him and let's get out of here!"

But just as the stranger reached for his dagger an arrow came screaming through the air.

"Quick! They're getting away!" shouted a shrill voice. Lady Gunnor and a group of soldiers were at the top of the steps.

Within seconds, arrows were flying everywhere. The stranger cried out. He'd been hit in the hand, and blood was dripping from an ugly wound. Guy pulled himself free and dashed towards Lady Gunnor and her men.

"Hold fire!" ordered Lady Gunnor, as Guy scrambled up the stairs to safety.

This was their chance. The archers had paused but it wouldn't be for long.

"Come here!" William shouted frantically, holding out his hand to the man who had so miraculously saved him. In a moment the stranger jumped onto the boat and Constance pushed away from the island, rowing as fast as she could.

They were quickly swallowed up by the fog. Arrows tore through the air, and plunged into the water only feet from the boat. But it was impossible for the marksmen to aim in the mist.

"Constance, let me help," said William, and they both tugged at the oars until the angry shouts grew fainter.

"Are you all right?" William asked the stranger once they were safely out of range and the only sound came from the lapping of water against the boat's hull and the oars creaking in their rowlocks.

He examined his hand.

"It's painful, but it looks worse than it is."

"Who are you?" asked William.

"I am Walter Fulbert... Your uncle."

William stared at the man, disbelievingly. "My uncle?"

"Yes – your mother, Herleve's, younger brother. It's been too many years since we last met."

23

"WHAT are you doing here?" asked William, as he rowed downstream.

His uncle dipped his hand in the river, cleaning the wound. A slight man with deep-set eyes, dark hair and a bushy beard, he was dressed in a brown cape, a faded tunic and leather boots – the clothes of a peasant farmer.

"You asked for help," Walter answered. "So your mother sent me. Yesterday, I waited for you in the churchyard at Pîtres."

"My guardian, Gilbert, insisted on going in my place," interrupted William.

"Yes. And I saw him murdered. There was nothing I could do. I was about to run for it myself when a young novice crept up and said he could help."

"A novice?" William was feeling more and more perplexed.

"He said he was a cousin of yours, Lord Nicholas of Fecamp is his name."

"Nicholas? What on earth was he doing there?"

"Waiting for you, your Grace. He said you were in trouble and together we planned how to get you off the island. Early this morning we stole the ferryman's boat and I rowed over. I was scouting the castle walls, looking for a possible way in when I heard a commotion and came to investigate."

"You came just in time, sir," said Constance.

"I could tell." Walter smiled.

"Where's Nicholas now?" asked William.

"Waiting on the far bank. Steer the boat that way but be quiet as we approach. We don't want anyone but him to know we're there."

The boat drifted silently in the fog. It was a strange feeling, floating along in the murkiness, but then suddenly and without warning, great branches of trees appeared and the boat ran aground in a muddy inlet, its hull crunching on stones. Walter put his finger to his lips, cupped his hands together and hooted once, and then twice more, sounding exactly like an owl.

Moments later Nicholas appeared from the forest. He waded into the river up to his knees, pushed the boat back into the water and jumped in.

"Let's go," he said, wringing water from his soaking brown robe. "Cotentin's men are all over the place. It's only the fog that's saving us from being seen."

Walter turned to William. "The river will carry us silently and if the fog holds we won't be seen for miles. So where would you like to go, your Grace? Where will you be safe?"

William looked blankly at his uncle. He hadn't a clue.

24

WILLIAM had been so occupied with getting off Vaudreuil that he hadn't had time to think about where he would go next. He didn't know who controlled the cities of Rouen or Falaise and he wasn't sure who his enemies were. Who could he trust other than the people sitting in this boat – Walter, Nicholas and Constance? There was one other person – his mother. *That's it*, he thought. *I must go to her.*

"Could you take me to Roche?" he asked.

Walter looked surprised.

"It's just a manor house, your Grace."

"It doesn't matter. My mother's there and I have nowhere else," said William simply.

"Then we'll float downriver, go ashore outside the village of La Londe and cut cross country. It will take three or four days at most, but before we set off there is something I should tell you, your Grace."

"What is it?" asked William sharply, for Walter sounded serious.

"Your mother's not well. She gave birth to another son in the autumn and has never recovered her strength."

"What's wrong with her?"

"The doctors say her humours are out of balance. They're bleeding her with leeches, but she was very weak when I left. We may not reach her in time."

It began to rain, great drops of water that soaked their clothes and dripped down their faces, but William didn't care. All he could think about was his sick mother and how he'd left it too late. Coming so soon after the deaths of Osbern and Gilbert, the news was too much. If only he'd tried to find her sooner.

When the little rowing boat pulled into a desolate cove just outside La Londe, Walter bound up his hand with a rag and told William, Constance and Nicholas to wait while he went into the village to get some food. William was so miserable he sank down on the muddy earth under a large oak tree.

The others came and sat next to him.

"I'm so sorry, your Grace," said Constance. "Is there anything I can do to help?"

William shook his head.

"Then I'd best be going. You don't need me tagging along. The more there are of us, the more chance there is of you being found."

"I should go too," said Nicholas. "I came to help because I overheard the monks at Evreux saying Lady Gunnor had switched sides. But now I should leave. A small group is far less likely to be noticed."

William suddenly realized how selfish he was being. Both Constance and Nicholas's predicaments were almost as bad as his own – they'd sacrificed everything to save him and he must do what he could for them.

"What are you talking about?" he said to Constance. "Where would you go?"

"I'll find work, your Grace."

"Where? You can't go back to Vaudreuil or your village. And you, Nicholas, you're in almost as much danger as me. You're a direct descendant of a duke, remember."

"But I don't *want* to be duke," protested Nicholas. "I promised your father, and I meant it."

"*I* know that, but others don't. Guy's after the duchy. He's not going to risk you being a rival. You must both come with me. We'll be safer together."

"I couldn't do that, your Grace," said Constance, looking horrified. "I'm only a maid and you're the duke … it wouldn't be fitting."

"Well, as your duke, I'm ordering you to stay. And there's another thing. There must be no more 'Your Graces' or we'll be found out immediately."

"Well, if you're ordering me," said Constance, sounding distinctly unsure, "then I suppose I must."

"Good," said William. "Nicholas?"

"I'll stay too."

Just then Walter emerged from the undergrowth, beckoning them to follow.

"There's a cattle market close to Roche this Saturday. I've brought five cows from a farmer in La Londe for us to trade. It'll be the perfect cover for us two."

"For the four of us," said William quickly. "Constance and Nicholas saved my life. I can't leave them behind."

"For the four of us," agreed Walter, "but remember, if anyone asks, we're a family and you, your Grace—"

"William," William corrected.

"William," continued his uncle, "you must change your clothes. You're far too conspicuous, dressed in those fancy things. I pulled these off a washing line – they're a bit damp but they'll do."

He threw over a patched pair of britches, a cloak woven from scratchy wool and a grey tunic which had been torn and poorly repaired.

"You really want me to wear these?" William wrinkled his nose at the shabby garments.

"Yes," said Walter firmly. "You must look like a farmer's boy or we'll never make it to Roche without being discovered. Now wait here while I find something for Nicholas."

William pulled on the clothes. Despite being pinched from a washing line they looked grubby and smelt awful – musty with a whiff of sweat and manure – but at least for now he was safe and amongst friends.

All day they drove the cattle south-west towards the village of Roche. The honey-coloured cows made slow, lumbering progress and stopped frequently to graze, but the travellers aroused little curiosity.

At first the countryside was lush and fertile and the

fields were neatly ploughed, ready for spring planting. But as they went further west this changed. Meadows were overgrown with weeds, homes were burnt out and many villages had been abandoned altogether. It was a dismal and depressing sight and the little party walked in gloomy silence.

Towards dusk, they came across a deserted house in a wood with a shabby cattle stall.

"We'll stop here for the night," said Walter.

William was relieved. He was soaking, his feet ached and he was exhausted, but when he opened the rotten door of the cottage, his spirits sank. The walls were covered with mould, the floor was rough earth and the place was filthy with rat droppings. Its previous occupants had clearly fled in a hurry, for drawers were left half-open and a cask of mildewed flour was spilt on the table.

"Perhaps we should try somewhere else," he said.

"No," said his uncle. "I know it's not what you're used to, William, but we're lucky to have found it. Come on."

After a meagre supper of stale bread and cheese, they settled as best they could in the musty, damp, forsaken building.

"All this misery can't be worth it," muttered Constance as they lay shivering, trying to get to sleep.

"What do you mean?" asked William.

"Nothing, sir."

"Tell me."

"I suppose I meant," she said tentatively, "it can't be

worth destroying people's homes so that one baron can own a bit more land than the next."

"It's always been that way," explained William. Most of his life there'd been fighting in Normandy and in the surrounding lands of Maine, Brittany and France. "For a time there's peace but then quarrels start again."

"But farmers and their children starve," said Constance sounding more confident, "or have to leave everything, like the poor people who ran from this place. It's not fair."

"You can't stop men fighting," said William wearily, gazing at the dying embers of a small fire. "It's impossible."

"Perhaps it will change one day," said Nicholas. "I heard some monks discussing something tried in Burgundy. It was called a Truce of God. To keep the peace between warring nobles, the bishops and the duke made a joint proclamation outlawing fighting during the days of Lent, Advent and Pentecost. That adds up to around a third of the year, and all the nobles had to take an oath promising to keep to the rules."

"And what happened?" asked William.

"From what the monks said, it worked for a while, but the duke wasn't strong enough to enforce it so the battles started again."

"See – I told you. Oaths don't count for much, particularly when people have no choice but to take them." William was thinking of the night in Falaise when his father had made all his nobles swear to serve William, and now look at him – sheltering in a derelict house from the very same men.

"Well, I still think something should be done," said Constance pensively. "Normandy can't continue like this."

ROCHE – MAY 1041

AFTER four days of hard travelling, it was close to midnight when they reached the village of Roche. Walter pointed out the flickering light from a small watchtower.

"That's it, William, that's your mother's home."

As they got closer, William could just make out the outline of the small thatched manor house, a barn and several outhouses all surrounded by a wooden fence. It seemed much smaller than he remembered all those years ago when he'd left for Falaise to answer his father's hurried summons, never suspecting that it would be seven years before he'd return.

He'd barely stepped through the door when a maid said, "Quick, your Grace, you must go to your mother at once. The doctor's been bleeding her, but he fears she won't be with us much longer."

The chamber was dark and shadowy. With a sense of foreboding, William crossed over to the bed where his mother lay. By the light of a solitary candle, he could see she was pale and painfully thin with hollow cheeks and colourless lips. On her bosom were three fat leeches, throbbing as they sucked at her warm blood.

"They're for her chest," explained the maid. "The doctor says her humours have too much phlegm. He's tried cutting her to drain off the bile but nothing worked – she just got sicker – and at the worst possible time. Her husband is away fighting."

"Don't worry, I'm here now," said William.

Trying not to look too closely at the gorging creatures, he leant over and kissed his mother's forehead. It was hot and her breathing was shallow and unnaturally fast. She stirred and opened her feverish eyes.

"William ... is that really you?"

He took her sickly hand and knelt by the bedside.

"Yes, Mother?"

Herleve lifted her head from the pillow, peered at him and then lay down again.

"You're so tall ... just like your father. I've missed your growing up."

"It's been seven years."

She nodded sadly. "I know. And I'm not going to live much longer. I hoped so much to see you before I go."

Her voice was frail and it took a great effort for her to speak.

"Now I'm here, you'll get better," said William.

She shook her head sadly.

"No, William. I get weaker every day. The doctors have

tried everything ... but I have so little strength left."

She coughed and struggled to catch her breath.

"Mother, you must rest," he said anxiously.

"There'll be time enough for that soon. First, I have something for you. Agatha."

The maid went to the far side of the room and returned with a small wooden box inlaid with intricate patterns of ivory.

With difficulty, Herleve propped herself up on her pillow and opened the box with the tiny key which hung from her necklace. William moved the candle closer. Inside, lying on blue velvet, was an exquisite pair of solid gold spurs.

"They belonged to your father."

"I remember," said William.

"He gave them to me for safekeeping when he left for Jerusalem. A pilgrim can't be dressed in such fine things. Take them."

William lifted the glinting spikes. They were heavier than he'd expected and cold to the touch. Each point was as sharp as a pin and letters were delicately engraved along the side.

"Do you know what it says?" asked William.

Herleve nodded and lay back down.

"They were a gift ... to your father from the King of France. Robert told me ... it spells 'Duke of Normandy'. They're yours now."

"I can't wear these," said William, picturing his father

in them all those years ago. He would feel absurd, an impostor.

"Yes you can. You're fourteen and a knight. You've earned them. Robert meant you to have them ... once you were ready. Now is the time for you to claim back the duchy from the traitors."

"How?" asked William.

"In Falaise you're in the land of my people. You have many friends ... I know you'll think of a way, and these spurs ... will help..." She closed her eyes.

"My lady is exhausted, your Grace," said Agatha. "You must let her rest."

As she showed William to his room she confided, "It won't be long now, sir. She was waiting for you, praying you'd come, reserving her strength as best she could. Now she can be at peace."

Back in his room, William sat on the bed staring at the brilliant spurs and going over and over the conversation with his mother ... *he was amongst friends here at Falaise ... he was ready ... he was a knight ... he must claim back the duchy.*

In the early hours of the morning, when the sky was still black, the news he'd been dreading came: his mother had died. But now at least he knew what he must do. The spurs were a sign. He had to risk everything or die trying. Somehow he must regain Normandy.

THAT same morning, just after dawn, William went to his uncle's room.

"I want you to find Gacé and summon him to Falaise Castle. Tell him his duke will see him there."

Walter, still in his nightshirt, stared at him open-mouthed.

"You want me to tell Gacé to go to Falaise, your Grace?"

"Yes. And tell him he must be there in three days. Where's Constance?"

"Sleeping in the back kitchen with the other maids."

When William reached the kitchen the servants were already attending to the first tasks of the day. The smell of baking bread filled the air, a fire was burning and two young girls were peeling vegetables. They curtseyed nervously when he appeared.

"Where's Constance?" he demanded.

"Out the back, your Grace," mumbled one of the girls.

He found her emptying a bucket of slop into a pig trough.

"Enough of that," said William. "I need the finest clothes you can find. I'm the duke and I have to look like one."

"What are you talking about, your Grace?" asked

Constance.

"I'm going to take Falaise. I can't keep running away and letting others rule the duchy. It's time I did it myself."

"But how?" said Constance. "You've got nobody to help you."

"That's not true. I've got you and Nicholas and Walter, and some of the people here at Roche. That's a start. And I'm going to get Gacé too."

"Gacé's your enemy!"

"I don't know that, I only know Cotentin is his. Gilbert said Gacé was ruthless but fair. If I can give him the chance to get his revenge, perhaps I can get him on my side, working for me."

"Don't you mean controlling you, like all the others?"

"Not this time. He must be a noble serving his duke – but he won't unless he believes I'm worthy. Now I understand why my father always wore these spurs. He had to *look* like a leader. Right now I look nothing of the sort, but if I had Falaise, I might."

"If Gacé does come, he could have you killed," said Constance. "You mustn't risk it."

"If I don't, I'll be killed anyway."

"But how on earth can you take the castle?"

"With these people's help." He pointed at the manor house and down the narrow valley. "If they want me as their duke I can do it. If not, I'm done for anyway. So now's the time to find out."

* * *

With Constance's help, William had everything he needed by lunchtime – chainmail, a shield, a metal helmet belonging to his father and a beautiful sword.

"Call everyone to the bailey," he ordered, "and get the stable boy to bring me the finest horse."

His fingers shaking, William tied his golden spurs round his ankles. *Stop it*, he told himself. He mustn't look afraid, he must stand straight, just as his father had, and look like a leader if he were to have any chance of pulling this off.

With his head held high, he walked out into the courtyard. A sleek white stallion was waiting for him, and his mother's household were gathered round, murmuring excitedly.

Walter called for quiet and then William spoke as calmly and forcefully as he could.

"Today is a sad day. My mother, your mistress, is dead. But the things she stood for – fairness, loyalty and a belief in what's right – are not. She taught me these things and I will not forget them. I know that many of you loved her. Well, I am her son and your duke. I have been betrayed by many enemies, but here, in her household, I hope I can find the support I'm due.

"Falaise is my home and the place of my birth. Along with the duchy, it was given to me by my father, Duke Robert, but traitors are trying to steal it away. You've seen the damage they've done, squabbling amongst themselves – there's no peace, farms are abandoned, people like you are starving. With your help I can bring an end to this. The nobles must be reminded of the oath they made to serve me. Will you come with me now to Falaise and demand this happens?"

Constance immediately stepped out of the crowd and stood beside William.

"I will, your Grace."

Nicholas was next. "I will, too."

He was swiftly followed by Walter.

"Is there anyone else?" asked William.

There was a terrible period during which the only sound was William's horse pawing the ground and snorting steam into the still, cold air. William knew that he was asking a lot.

At last a young girl stepped forward. It was Agatha, his mother's maid. "I will follow his golden spurs," she said quietly. "I know it was the dying wish of my mistress."

Then a scullery boy stepped forward. "Me too. Mistress Herleve was good and kind, and he is her son."

"I'll come," said a blacksmith, his ruddy face smeared with soot. "He's the rightful heir and the spitting image of his father."

And then person after person joined, until the whole of Herleve's household, a crowd of around fifty people, was lined up behind William.

"Let's go and win Falaise!" he commanded.

The parade of men and women walked out of the bailey and along the grassy track. At each hamlet along the way, villagers came running, curious at the sight of William and his band of followers marching behind him, waving cloaks, banners and even branches, and shouting, "Hail, William, son of Herleve!" or, "Long live the duke!"

In no time the message spread.

"The duke has come to bring peace to Normandy!"

"His mother was one of us!"

"He's our duke!"

By the time they reached Falaise, the crowd had swelled to hundreds of people. The great stone castle, with its forbidding high walls, towered above them, perching unnaturally on top of a huge jagged rock.

"Wait here," William commanded the crowd. He jumped down from his horse, walked alone up the steep track to the great castle and hammered on the door.

"Who's there?" asked a frightened voice from within.

"Your duke. Open up."

The door creaked open an inch, and an ancient, stooped man peered out.

"Your Grace, after all these years, you've come home," he said with tears in his eyes. It was the very same warden who'd shown William into the Great Hall on the night he and his mother had been summoned to Falaise by Duke Robert.

"Yes, I've come home," said William. "Instruct your men to put down their weapons, make space in the bailey for my followers, and when Gacé comes tell him his duke awaits."

FALAISE CASTLE – MAY 1041

"YOUR Grace, Lord Gacé and his men have arrived," reported the castle warden three days later. "They appeared in the night as if by magic – hundreds of them, far too many to fit in the bailey. They're camping outside the castle."

"Summon a council," said William, "and tell Gacé I'll see him at midday."

"Are you sure you're doing the right thing?" asked Nicholas, looking out of a window at Gacé's men gathering below. "His soldiers are everywhere. He has the place surrounded."

"I'll find out at midday," said William. "Wish me luck."

Exactly as the bell chimed the hour, William entered the grand chamber. He was dressed as a warrior, a great sword hanging from his waist and his father's gold spurs round his ankles. The warden had cobbled together a small band of trumpeters to herald him and an even smaller number of gentlemen and nobles from the surrounding towns and villages. *It's not much of a show of support*, thought William, *but it's a start.*

Gacé was waiting in the middle of the room with ten of his followers, all battle-hardened knights. With his missing left eye and severe grey tunic and britches, he was a sombre sight.

"You summoned me?" said Gacé.

William noted that Gacé did not call him "Your Grace".

"Yes, my Lord. As I'm sure you know, Cotentin is leading a rabble of men to overthrow me. You were one of my father's most trusted advisers, a great landowner and a renowned soldier. As one of my leading nobles, I'm looking to you to help me defeat him."

"Why should I risk my men to do that when your dukedom is all but over?"

"Because Cotentin has Vicomte Guy of Burgundy."

Gacé looked gratifyingly shocked. He understood the significance of this news. If Cotentin installed Guy as duke, then he would have everything. Only the duke could grant land, only the duke could sanction the building of a castle, only the duke could make laws. The Normans would never accept Cotentin as duke, for he had no blood claim, but they might accept Guy and if they did, Gacé, Cotentin's enemy, would pay as high a price as William.

"I remember your oath of allegiance to me," continued William, "and I believe you are a man of honour. So far you have only raised an army to protect your land from a traitor. Go further. Help me bring peace to the duchy, and I will reward you well."

"How?" asked Gacé. "You have nothing."

"I am still the duke. I can give land to whomever I choose. If we defeat Cotentin I promise his lands will pass to you. I will also appoint you my chief adviser and commander of my men."

"Cotentin has much of western Normandy."

"And soon it could be yours."

"What will become of him?" asked Gacé.

"That will be up to you. But Vicomte Guy is mine."

Gacé paused, considering gravely everything that William had said.

"I must consult with my men," he said at last.

William waited anxiously, knowing his future hung in the balance.

Finally Gacé turned round, approached William and knelt.

"You make a strong case, your Grace, and I would be honoured to serve you. But the campaign will be long and hard. Cotentin has many men on his side."

"I know," said William. "But we have Falaise. From here we must recapture the duchy and this time I *will* prevail. There can be no refuge anywhere for my enemies. Even if it takes years we must seek them out and expel them. They must learn there's no place for them to hide."

PART III

FIVE YEARS LATER
LESTRE, WESTERN NORMANDY
AUTUMN 1046

28

As the autumn sun was setting, a group of twenty knights came clattering over the drawbridge into the bailey of Lestre Castle. Like the rest of the fort it was unimpressive – a muddy courtyard, littered with piles of wood, a tatty forge and rundown outhouses.

Constance, wrapped in a warm shawl, was waiting by a rickety shed.

"How was it, your Grace?" she called to William, who was riding a black horse at the head of his men.

He dismounted and came over to her, looking thoughtful.

"Almost too good to be true."

Since that day, five long years ago, when Gacé had agreed to become his chief councillor, William's situation in Normandy had begun to improve. Together, they'd ridden through the duchy rallying supporters and attacking rebels. There had been many fierce battles and under Gacé's expert instruction William had learnt how to conduct a siege, when to use archers, cavalry or lancers, and how to spot an ambush. And month by month, bit by bit, more and more territory came under William's control.

Finally, he'd returned triumphantly to Rouen, his capital, and pardoned the last of the rebels in return for a promise of peace. After years of war, farmers went back to their fields, and new churches and monasteries were built – and yet, in his heart, William knew all was not well. Although he now made the laws, granted land, dispensed justice and settled disputes, his grip on power was fragile – and the reason was his cousin, Guy! Infuriatingly, though Guy had been defeated in battle, both he and Cotentin had managed to escape.

They were rumoured to be sheltering in the remote mountains of western Normandy. Scouts picked up tales of them offering fantastic bribes for the heads of either the duke or his chief councillor. Then one terrible day in the spring, Gacé was assassinated – an arrow in his chest – and William realized he had to act. He must find Guy and Cotentin and deal with them, once and for all. So he gathered a band of loyal knights and friends, asked Constance to supervise the accompanying servants, and set off.

For the past four months they'd travelled further and further west, spending the days touring villages and the nights in the nearest fort, in a seemingly endless quest for some sign of William's enemies. But frustratingly, in all this time they'd picked up no clues as to where Guy and Cotentin were. It was as though they had disappeared into thin air.

"What do you think, Nicholas, sir?" asked Constance.

Nicholas slipped down from his horse and brushed straw from his austere brown habit.

"I think William's worrying about nothing. Every village welcomed us with gifts of ham and wine. I've never seen anything like it."

"That's because you spend most of the year in a priory," said William. He'd recently appointed his cousin to the prestigious position of Abbot of Saint-Ouen and this was Nicholas's first journey round Normandy for many months. "I'm telling you, something's not right."

"But you can't seriously think Guy and Cotentin are around here, your Grace," said Nicholas. "A scout would have heard something. They must have fled to England like Lady Alice. Sir, you must accept that you won't find them this year. We should go home to Rouen before winter sets in and come again in spring."

"No," said William stubbornly. "We must carry on. I won't stop until I've found them."

* * *

The next evening William led his weary troop of knights, soldiers and servants into Valognes, the most westerly castle in Normandy. It was an isolated, ramshackle place at the end of a long chalky road which wound its way through dense pine forests and then up a steep hill. The small fort was built on the crown of this mound. It had a wooden keep, a courtyard with stabling, and outhouses, all encircled by a timber fence.

A warden was waiting by the castle gates. He was elderly, with a stooped back and an angry rash on his neck. His hands shook as the duke approached.

"My Lord, your messenger only brought me news of your visit yesterday," he said nervously. "I've had no time to tell my master to return, or prepare a feast."

"Don't worry," said William. "All we need is a place to stay the night and a simple supper. We'll be leaving first thing in the morning."

"As you like, your Grace," said the warden, uneasily licking his lips over and over. "Let me show you to your chamber."

With painful slowness he led William up several flights of stairs to a damp room at the top of the keep. As he opened the door a nest of starlings flapped round and fluttered off out of the window.

"I'm afraid it's the best we have, your Grace."

Although the room was worn and draughty, the bed looked comfortable enough and after another long day in the saddle, that was all William cared about.

"This will be fine," he said. "Have the cook bring me some ham, cheese and bread. I'll eat here."

After finishing his meagre supper, William stretched out on the bed in his britches and tunic, not bothering to undress, and fell into an exhausted sleep, but it seemed almost no time had passed when he was woken by knocking at the door. He opened his eyes. The room was pitch-black. It must be the middle of the night. Who on earth would be waking him now?

Groggily he called out, "Who is it?"

"Constance. Quick!" She sounded terrified.

Instantly William was fully awake. He hurriedly lit a candle and unbolted the door.

"What is it?" he asked.

Dressed only in a night shift, with a shawl thrown around her shoulders and her long brown hair unbrushed, was Constance. Standing next to her was a short bald man. It was one of William's scouts and from the look on his face something was terribly wrong.

"Your Grace, they're coming to kill you. You must flee!"

"Who's coming to kill me? What are you talking about?" said William.

"I've come straight from Bayeux," said the scout breathlessly. "I was sleeping in a stable there when I was disturbed by two men. I was about to tell them to be quiet when I realized they were discussing some sort of ambush, so I followed them all the way to the town square. Your Grace, although it was close to midnight, it was full of soldiers and a young gentleman, not much older than you, was saying by dawn he'd be Duke and they'd be rich and it would be a famous victory. I grabbed my horse and galloped here, but they can't be far behind."

"What did their leader look like?" asked William.

The scout thought for a moment.

"Fair, quite short and stocky with a long pointed nose."

"Guy!" said William. At last he'd come out of hiding.

"Constance, wake the steward. Tell him to get the knights ready."

"Your Grace, you can't do that," said the scout emphatically. "I haven't told you the worst of it. That man – Guy, you called him – promised his soldiers that your men here at Valognes wouldn't put up a fight. He said, 'They'll open the castle gates for us.'"

"What does that mean?" asked Constance.

"You're surrounded by traitors," said the scout. "He boasted that half the knights here are in his pay. I didn't even dare disturb the guards when I came in. I tied my horse up in the forest and climbed over the wall where it's lowest, rather than risk being seen."

"What are you going to do, your Grace?" asked Constance frantically. "Could we lock the traitors in the dungeon?"

"We don't even know who they are," said William grimly, "and we don't have time to find out."

Hurriedly, he threw his father's golden spurs, a shirt, a couple of rolls of bread and a hunk of cheese left over from last night's supper into a leather satchel and grabbed his cloak. He might have only minutes to spare before Guy and his men arrived. The only thing to do was flee and as quickly as possible.

"What are you doing?" asked Constance.

"We've got to get away. Come on."

"You two go," said the scout. "If I stay and bolt the door it might fool them into thinking you're still inside. It'll give you more time. Go on! Go!"

Quickly William and Constance crept away, not daring to wake anyone except Nicholas, the only person in the castle they knew they could trust.

Moments later all three met in the bailey. Nicholas had thrown on his abbot's habit and Constance had hurriedly pulled on a long woollen skirt over her nightdress. William was in yesterday's mud-spattered clothes. There had been no time to grab anything apart from William's satchel with the precious spurs.

"Quick!" he said. "Let's saddle the horses and get out of here before the guards wake."

They hurried to the stable, but to their horror it was empty.

"What's going on?" asked Nicholas.

"Someone's released them," said William. "Someone who's working for Guy."

"Then we're stuck here?" said Constance, panic in her voice.

Just then there was a far-off cry. The night was crisp and clear, stars twinkling in the black sky, but in the distance, beyond the wooden fence, was an eerie, orange glow. It had to be the torches of Guy and his men.

"They're almost here," said Nicholas. "We're trapped. Without horses, there's no way out."

VALOGNES – AUTUMN 1046

"WAIT," said Constance. "You heard the scout, your Grace. There's a horse tied up in the forest behind the castle."

"It can't possibly take three of us," said William.

"It doesn't need to take us all," said Constance. "It's you they want. You're the one that needs to get away."

"I'm not leaving without both of you," said William firmly.

"No. Constance is right," said Nicholas. "They're corrupt and cruel and it's your duty to stop them, but if you take us with you, we'll only slow you down."

"Don't be stupid," said William. "We'll make it somehow."

Just then an arrow whipped through the still, cold air. William pushed Constance and Nicholas back into the empty stable as the night watchman shouted, "We're under attack!" and began clanging a bell to wake the castle.

Suddenly horses came thundering out of the darkness towards the fort. Sleepy men poured out from the keep, hastily pulling on armour and clothes, shouting, gesticulating and unsheathing their swords, but it was just as the scout had said – half of William's men were fighting their own side.

More arrows started raining down and then hundreds of soldiers came smashing through the castle gates, screaming and thrusting swords and spears.

"I hate it," said Constance, shaking her head. "Why are there always these endless battles? So many people will be killed before it's over."

William peered round the stable door. Constance was right. He didn't dare tell her what he could see: hundreds of men, slashing and stabbing each other. One man had lost an arm, another's stomach was bleeding hideously, and several knights had gruesome cuts on their faces and hands. Into the middle of this commotion rode Guy and Cotentin. William hadn't seen either of them for over five years but they were unmistakable – Guy, with his blond hair and sharp nose, and Cotentin, flamboyantly dressed in a green velvet cloak over his armour, almost too heavy for his horse. William couldn't believe they were only feet away from him. In the darkness and chaos they hadn't yet spotted him, but it wouldn't take long.

"Find the duke! Search the castle!" shouted Guy excitedly. "He's in there somewhere."

"I know where," a man called out. It was the elderly castle warden.

No wonder he'd looked so nervous the previous

evening, thought William bitterly. He must have known this attack was coming. William couldn't believe how stupid he'd been. He'd sensed something was wrong and yet he'd been so determined to root out Guy and Cotentin that he hadn't stopped for reinforcements or returned in the spring, as Nicholas had suggested. Instead he'd allowed himself to be drawn further and further west into his enemies' territory, and now they'd trapped him where he was weakest.

"Good work. Where is he, then?" asked Guy.

"Locked in a chamber at the top of the keep, sir. He's bolted the door."

"Right, you men guard the gate," instructed Guy, pointing at a group of burly soldiers. "I don't want him getting away. And you lot, come with me."

He jumped off his horse and ran up the motte to the tower, followed by his men, a puffing Cotentin and the limping warden.

William knew it wouldn't take them long to break down the door and discover the scout in his chamber, and then they'd search the castle until they found him. Sheltering in the stable was hopeless. They had to find another way out.

"Hide under the straw, your Grace," implored Constance frantically.

"No," said William. "It's the first place they'll look. That scout got over the wall. We'll do the same and then his horse will have to do. Follow me."

Staying in the shadow of the fence, William led them to the back of the bailey, as far away from the guarded castle gates and the rebels as possible.

"But how are we going to get out here?" asked Nicholas, looking up at the fence.

"It's too high, your Grace," said Constance. "We'll never do it."

"Yes we will," said William, but when he looked up he saw the fence was well over seven feet high – a good foot above him and considerably taller than Nicholas and Constance.

"Where is he?" It was Guy roaring in frustration. "Search the castle! Look everywhere!"

"Quick, we've got to give it a go," said William desperately. "Constance, come on. I'll lift you."

"No, you go first," said Nicholas. "You're in britches. I can't climb in this habit and Constance's skirt is even worse. You're the tallest. I'll give you a leg up and you can pull us from the top."

In no time William was balancing precariously on the fence, one leg either side. He could hear the soldiers getting closer and closer, stabbing piles of hay, searching the tatty outhouses and calling his name.

"Constance, you next," said William, leaning down to grab her hand.

Just then a man shouted, "I've seen him!"

"Your Grace, go!" implored Nicholas. "There's no time for us."

And before William could stop them, Nicholas and Constance shoved his foot upwards, toppling him over the fence. He landed with a thud on the ground, then rolled uncontrollably down the steep hill, his satchel tumbling after him.

He scrambled to his feet and stared up at the castle, but it was hopeless – he'd never be able to scale the barricade from this side. Nicholas and Constance had saved him, and there was nothing he could do for them.

"Get on your horses! Get after him!" ordered a voice. "He's escaping."

Suddenly William came to his senses. He had to use the chance they had so bravely given him. He picked up the satchel and ran towards the forest, frantically searching in the gloom for a horse. After a couple of frenzied minutes he found a chestnut mare saddled, and tied to a tree, and peacefully chomping grass. Quickly he put his foot in the stirrup, pulled himself up and galloped away into the enveloping shadows. He'd escaped Guy's clutches, but he was a fugitive in his own land once more.

WILLIAM galloped deeper into the woods, glancing over his shoulder for one last look at Valognes. The wooden fort was ablaze, flames licking the top of the tower, and he could hear pitiful screams. Somewhere in the middle of that hell were Nicholas and Constance. He couldn't bear to think what was happening to them, but he was certain of one thing – he would never see them again.

Don't look back! You can't look back! he told himself as he spurred his horse. He followed a bridle path through the pine trees of the lonely forest, but he had no idea where he was going. He only knew he had to get as far from Valognes as possible.

In the moonlight, the trees cast ghostly shadows and every rock looked perfect for an ambush. *Calm down*, William told himself, but he knew he was right to be worried. Guy and Cotentin's men would be scouring the land searching for him, and they knew this territory better than he did.

The forest began to thin and he rode out into a clearing. Ahead of him the path forked. He pulled his reins to slow the mare down and studied the night sky, searching for the North Star. There it was, twinkling at the end of the

Plough. So the left path must lead west, deeper into Guy's territory, and the right path east, home to Falaise.

He was about to head east when there was a commotion of flapping wings and the loud cawing of crows. A great cloud of black birds rose from the forest. His pursuers were getting closer.

He wanted to spur his horse, but it was pointless. The mare was exhausted from the long ride from Bayeux and this wild dash. Frantically he looked for somewhere to hide. To his left was a thicket of dense pine trees. His heart racing, he led her through the prickly branches, praying her hoof marks wouldn't show in the long grass.

Moments later two riders pounded into the clearing and stopped at the fork in the path.

Go on! thought William. *Don't stop here!* The slightest sound and he would be discovered. He stroked the mare comfortingly, willing her to be quiet.

"Which way would he have run?"

The voice was unmistakable. William peered through the branches. Guy was patting his horse's neck and talking to a soldier – Tesson, one of William's own knights. William couldn't believe *he* was a traitor. He'd knighted him only months before. If someone like Tesson could turn against him, how many more were on Guy's side?

"He can't have got this far by foot," said Tesson.

"Then he's not on foot," retorted Guy tetchily. "My men have searched the castle but somehow he must have got hold of a horse."

"I drove them all from the stable," protested Tesson.

"Clearly, not well enough. Now which way? I'd say east to Falaise, hoping to raise his peasant army again," said Guy. "But don't worry, I've got allies waiting there and anywhere else he might show up. Come on."

The two men flicked their reins, spurred their horses hard in the flank and were off, taking the very path William had planned to take only minutes earlier. But it wasn't safe for him to go to Falaise or Rouen. Guy had said he had traitors lying in wait there. *So where can I go?* thought William angrily. *Is everywhere in Normandy against me?* And then he had an idea. Normandy might be dangerous but there was a land that had sheltered him years ago. France. Gilbert had said that King Henry was not to be trusted, but in his bones William had always felt he was wrong. It was time to back his own judgment. Somehow he must get to Paris and claim his due – support from his suzerain, King Henry of France.

PARIS, FRANCE – AUTUMN 1046

"A boy claiming to be the Duke of Normandy requests an audience, your Majesty."

William was waiting outside King Henry's private chamber. He was filthy and exhausted after a desperate, lonely dash across Normandy and into France. He could hear the incredulous tone of the herald. It had taken all of his powers of persuasion to get this far into the castle. If it weren't for the gold spurs he'd put on when he reached the outskirts of Paris, he would never have made it.

"The Duke of Normandy? Are you sure?" rumbled a deep, familiar voice.

"No, your Majesty, but he's wearing Duke Robert's spurs and he swears blind he's Sir William."

"What does he look like?" asked the king, sounding doubtful.

"Tall, red-haired, thin as a beanpole and looking in need of a meal."

"Let him in."

William fell to his knees as the door was opened wide

and kissed the hem of Henry's lavish fur cloak.

"You told me to come to you, my protector, if I ever needed help, and now I do."

"Let me see your face," ordered the king.

William looked up into Henry's dark brown eyes.

"My goodness, it *is* you. After all these years, you've come back. But look at the state of you. Tell me, how did you get here?"

Briefly, William spoke of his journey and his troubles. He told the king of the murder of Gilbert and Osbern and the treachery of Guy and Cotentin.

"Your Majesty, you told me you once came to my father with little to your name, and he treated you with honour and helped you recover your throne. Will you do the same for me?"

"You want me to lead an army into Normandy?" asked the king.

William shook his head. That was the last thing he wanted. Ever since he'd become duke others had fought his battles – Gilbert and Lord Gacé. This time it had to be him. He must show his nobles once and for all that he was their leader. He was the one they must fear and respect. He was the one they must not defy. He was certain many of them had deserted him because he was a bastard and the son of a peasant. Now they would see he deserved to be duke, not just because his father said so but because he could command an army, vanquish his enemies and bring peace to his land.

"Thank you, your Majesty," he said, "but no. *I* must lead the army or I'll never be respected in Normandy, and I won't deserve to be. I'm asking only for men. When I return there, I'm sure many more will join. Will you help me, sire?"

It took no time for the king to respond.

"A rebellion against you is a rebellion against me," said Henry firmly. "You have come to your suzerain and bravely demanded your rights. How could I refuse?"

ROUEN, NORMANDY – JANUARY 1047

FOUR months after his lonely ride from Valognes, William crossed back into Normandy with three thousand men under his command. Some were loyal Normans who'd travelled to Paris when news spread of his impending return, and others were French soldiers sent by King Henry. They were an impressive sight – knights on horses with ornate swords and colourful shields, archers with bows slung over their shoulders, infantrymen trudging along with spears, and, behind them all, hundreds of carts loaded with food, beer, tents and blankets.

William pushed on, deeper and deeper into Normandy, until one cold January afternoon he spotted the familiar spires and walls of the great city of Rouen on the horizon. This would be his first test and he had no idea what awaited him. Would Guy and Cotentin have retreated to the west, or would they be here, preparing for a final confrontation?

"Your Grace, do you want to stop for the night or

should we keep going?" asked Walter. William's uncle had been one of the first Normans to arrive in Paris.

William knew it would be madness to attack when the light was fading. They must use the cover of darkness to study the castle and its surrounding terrain, and strike first thing in the morning.

"No. We'll rest here," he said, "but bring me ten men so we can have a look round Rouen and see how they're planning to defend it."

As dusk approached William rode out of the camp. Behind him a canvas city had sprung up. There were hundreds of tents and campfires, and the delicious smell of sizzling pork filled the air. But ahead was the fortress, with walls over twelve feet thick, a moat, drawbridge and forbidding battlements. It would take all his skills to capture it.

As William got closer he noticed that the parapets were shimmering.

"Do you see that?" he asked Walter, pointing ahead.

His uncle gazed up.

"They're flags, aren't they?"

They rode nearer. All along the ramparts people were waving sheets, standards, blankets and even cloaks, and now they could hear chanting – "Duke William! Duke William!" The noise was getting louder every moment.

"Well, they know I'm here," said William grimly, "but I'm not sure what they want."

"Could they be surrendering?" asked Walter, puzzled

by the din and the banners.

William studied the fluttering colours: reds, oranges, blues, greens and pinks. They looked so joyful rippling in the breeze, more like a carnival than a town preparing to capitulate – could it be that Rouen, his old capital, was welcoming him home?

"No," he said excitedly. "They're not surrendering, they're celebrating our return. Walter, send your knights back to the camp. Tell them to get the men ready to march into town. You and I will go and find out who's behind this."

As William rode across the drawbridge, the sound of hundreds of people chanting his name was deafening. He'd never had such a greeting in all his life.

"The tyrants have gone!"

"No more looting now the duke's returned!"

"Our homes will be safe!"

People crowded round him, chanting and dancing with delight. He grabbed the arm of a young woman.

"Which of the nobles organized this?"

She laughed and shook her head. "It wasn't a noble, your Grace. It was a monk."

"Which monk?" William shouted over the roar of the crowd.

"The Abbot of Saint-Ouen."

"There is no Abbot of Saint-Ouen," said William, thinking of the terrible day he'd abandoned Nicholas and Constance at Valognes.

"Yes, there is," said the girl confidently. "He returned

to his monastery the day Lord Guy and Lord Cotentin marched their men out of the city. That Sunday he preached in the cathedral that you'd come back and bring peace to the land and that we should get banners ready to welcome you."

"What does this monk look like?" William asked, suddenly hopeful.

"He's not much older than you. Abbot Nicholas is his name. I dare say he's in the monastery now."

"Nicholas, how on earth did you survive?" asked William.

They were standing under a stone arch in the cloisters of Saint-Ouen, just beyond the city walls. Outside, the crowds could still be heard celebrating the duke's return.

Nicholas answered William's question by holding up the plain silver cross on a thin chain which hung round his neck.

"Guy's men refused to kill or imprison a man of the church, so he had to let me go. But Valognes was destroyed, there was nothing – no food, horses or shelter – just a smouldering ruin, and I think Guy was certain I'd die in such an isolated place. But I managed to make it to the monastery at Montebourg where the monks hid me. When I heard of your return I knew I had to get back here. I arrived two days ago."

"And Constance?" said William eagerly. "Did she get

away too?"

Nicholas shook his head sadly. He looked drawn, as if he couldn't bear to be reminded of what he'd witnessed. At last he said quietly, "Your Grace, you don't want to hear what they did to her. All I know is that Guy doesn't deserve to live after that."

William sank down onto a stone step, his head in his hands. Constance had been so kind, loyal and brave. He would make Guy pay, if it was the last thing he did.

"Where is he?" he asked.

"He and Cotentin are waiting for you at Val-es-Dunes, near Caen," said Nicholas. "It's in the west."

"Then that's where I'm going," said William. "but in the meantime there's something I need you to do."

"What, your Grace?" asked Nicholas.

"You remember when we travelled from Vaudreuil to Roche – on the first night we camped in a derelict house and you mentioned an agreement that was tried in Burgundy?"

"The Truce of God."

"Yes. In memory of Constance we must make such a truce, here in Normandy. Summon the archbishops and abbots. Go to the Pope if necessary, but have a document ready by the time the battle is over. I'm going to persuade my nobles to sign it, not because I order them to, but because it is something they truly believe in. That's the only way it will succeed."

VAL-ES-DUNES – JANUARY 1047

JUST after dawn, when the mist was still clinging to the ground, William led his men to a field outside the tiny hamlet of Val-es-Dunes. The rebel army was waiting for him.

There were three neat lines of soldiers, archers and knights on horseback and behind that, next to a yellow and red standard, were Guy and Cotentin. The meadow was large, flat and frosty, its grass frozen and glimmering in the bright sun. It was surrounded by forest on three sides and its fourth boundary was the meandering River Orne. Usually it was a peaceful, lonely spot but not this morning, for the fight for the control of Normandy was about to begin.

William, riding a beautiful, dappled grey-and-white horse, was dressed for battle in a chainmail tunic with mail sleeves and chausses to protect his legs. An iron helmet covered his face, and his father's spurs were tied to his ankles. Holding a wooden club, an ancient symbol of authority, high in the air, he led his men to the far side of the field. Although outwardly calm, he was desperately nervous. This was the first time he'd led his men into battle alone, without Gacé at his side. He missed the old warrior's shrewdness and experience, but, he kept telling himself, he'd done all the preparation he could. At dawn, just as Gacé had taught him, he'd stolen into the field to study the battle terrain and he was convinced that Guy and Cotentin had made a tactical error. They were too close to the river. With luck, if William's men swung hard to the left, they'd get trapped by it. His future, and the future of his duchy, rested upon it.

The horse, sensing his rider's tension, became skittish, and William stroked his neck to calm him before trotting out in front of his men.

"Today," he said, praying that his voice would not quaver and betray his nerves, "we are fighting not for ourselves, but for Normandy. We are fighting to rid this land of tyrants and thieves. We are fighting for peace. Everyone must play their part if we are to prevail. We must be brave, resolute and determined. We must keep going until we've defeated them. I ask one thing of you and one thing only: leave Vicomte Guy to me."

With that William took a deep breath, turned, spurred his horse and charged forwards towards the left-hand side of the rebel lines. Behind him there was a roar as the infantry followed, screaming at the top of their voices.

Spears, rocks and arrows rained down, smashing

shields, piercing armour and sending men tumbling to the ground. William threw himself at man after man, slashing with his sword. A knight caught his cheek with the tip of his sword, pushing him off balance. The pain was shocking and he had to fight to stay on his horse. He felt the blood running down his cheek.

"The duke's hurt!"

"William's wounded!"

He could hear panic in his men's voices so he snatched off his helmet to show them he was all right. "It's nothing," he shouted, "just a scratch," and then he pushed on relentlessly, desperate to fight his way through to Guy and Cotentin.

The meadow was a scene of carnage. The wounded lay groaning amongst piles of dead and from everywhere came screams of agony and rage, but the rebels were slowly being pushed back, just as William had planned, and trapped by the banks of the river. Several fell into the water and, unable to swim in their heavy armour, were carried away by the current.

"Keep going, men!" yelled William. "We've nearly done it."

And as more and more rebels thrashed frantically in the freezing black waters of the Orne, the battle was turning into a rout.

Suddenly William spotted Guy over by the riverbank. With one last effort he pushed himself forward through a throng of fighting men.

"Guy!" he shouted at the top of his voice. "This is for Constance!"

He jumped off his horse and charged, but before he could reach him, Guy, panic-struck, waded into the river's reed banks.

"Who's running now?" William screamed. "Who's got nowhere to hide?"

He grabbed the bow of the nearest soldier but it was too late. Guy sank below the surface, weighed down by his chainmail and the mud. The River Orne had done William's job for him.

"Where's Cotentin?" he shouted. "Does anyone know where he is?"

"Drowned, your Grace," shouted a knight, "like so many others."

The news flew round the battlefield. The rebels had been defeated and were begging for mercy. William had won.

He raised his mace, waiting for silence from his exhausted warriors.

"Victory is ours!" he shouted to a resounding cheer. "Help the wounded and bury the dead, and then come to the city of Caen. Whether you are on my side or a rebel you must celebrate, for I swear this will be the last conflict in our land."

* * *

That night William summoned every noble in Normandy to a council outside the city walls. They crowded round a hastily erected wooden platform. Behind them were soldiers and, beyond that, hundreds of farmers, peasants, and traders from the town. As William pushed his way through to the stage many patted him on the back and congratulated him on his victory. It was something he had never experienced before – his people looking at him with frank admiration and respect – and it was just what he needed if the Truce was to have any chance of working.

William climbed onto the stage. He was still in the clothes he'd worn that day on the battlefield, his cheek smeared with dried blood. Nicholas was waiting for him with every senior churchman in Normandy.

"I trust you've got it," he said quietly.

"Yes, your Grace," said Nicholas, holding up a rolled parchment of vellum. "The Truce is written here and every churchman will enforce it."

"You've done well. Now let's see if I can persuade them to agree to it."

William moved to the front of the stage, waiting for the crowd to quieten, and then began the most important speech of his life.

"For twelve years since my father left for his pilgrimage to the Holy Land, Normandy has been at war not with an enemy but with itself," he said in a loud, clear voice that carried easily across the vast crowd. "The duchy is exhausted. We've all lost friends, homes and family. But now it must stop. There must be no more battles. You, the people, are paying too heavy a price for the endless feuds between nobles, and I will not allow it to continue."

There was a tremendous cheer from the crowd. William had struck home.

"I have therefore asked Abbot Nicholas of Saint-Ouen to prepare the first Truce of God for Normandy. This Truce forbids any baron, knight or soldier from taking up arms during the seasons of Advent, Lent, Easter and Pentecost. Furthermore, it outlaws fighting between Wednesday night and Monday morning. Any man that promises to obey the Truce and then breaks this law, whatever the provocation and however wealthy and noble, will be excommunicated by the church. You see here every abbot, archbishop and bishop in the duchy. These men will not allow anyone who breaks this agreement to enter a chapel in Normandy. They will not be permitted a Christian burial and their children will not be baptized. The only exception to this is your duke, and I swear I will only break it to keep peace in this land."

He beckoned to Nicholas to bring over the rolled-up parchment.

"The Abbot has the Truce of God but also a holy relic – the finger of his monastery's founder, Saint Ouen. I am asking each you tonight to swear on this relic that you will abide by the Truce, but you may only do so on one condition – that you do it willingly. I will force nobody. The choice must be yours, for the oath will only be of value if you believe in it and will adhere to it. In the past, too many solemn promises have been broken."

He surveyed the crowd, willing them to understand how serious he was. If the nobles signed the Truce he intended to hold them to it ruthlessly, so that his subjects, good people like Constance, could live in peace.

A soldier in clanking armour was the first to climb the steps onto the wooden stage. He pulled off his helmet in front of William and fell to his knees. It was Tesson, the knight who had betrayed him at Valognes.

"Your Grace, I'm ashamed to say I fought on the side of Guy and Cotentin, but I'm weary of battle and I'm sorry. Please forgive me and let me swear first."

William nodded, knowing his enemies as well as his friends must honour the Truce of God if his plan was to work. Tesson took the relic and the parchment and repeated Nicholas's words simply and fervently:

"I solemnly swear on the bones of Saint Ouen that I will abide by this holy Truce of God."

The crowd roared its approval and then another warrior followed, and then many more. Each man sounded more eager and enthusiastic than the last. It gave William hope. This *was* different from the oath extracted so grudgingly by his father.

He studied the excited crowd gathering to climb onto the stage. It seemed every knight in the land was impatient to take the pledge. Now William was confident he would bring peace and prosperity to his land. He would make it great, for at last he was truly in charge of his duchy and had earned his title – Duke of Normandy.

THE END

WHAT HAPPENED NEXT

The defeat of Guy and Cotentin at the Battle of Val-es-Dunes and the signing of the Truce of God were not the end of William's troubles, but they did represent a key turning point in his fortunes. From that victory onwards William stopped being a beleaguered duke and became one who was increasingly feared and respected.

By 1050, William's position in Normandy was sufficiently secure for him to seek a wife. He approached the powerful King Baldwin the Fifth of Flanders and asked for his daughter Matilda's hand in marriage. She declared she would rather become a nun than marry a bastard. William was so incensed that one day, when she was leaving church, he threw her to the ground, tore her clothes and rode off. Despite this inauspicious start, Matilda and William did marry and together had four sons and five daughters. They must have made an odd pair. At five feet and ten inches, William was extremely tall for the age, whereas Matilda was tiny at just over four feet.

In 1051, William sailed to England to visit his cousin, King Edward the Confessor. This was the same Edward who had sheltered in Normandy when the Danes had invaded his kingdom. William's visit was to prove a turning point in history, for during his stay in London the childless Edward the Confessor declared William heir to the English throne.

Thirteen years later, in 1064, Harold of Wessex, a brother-in-law of Edward the Confessor, was sailing in the English Channel when his ship was blown off course. Fatefully, it landed in northern Normandy. By this time King Edward the Confessor was elderly and unwell, and Harold was a potential challenger for the English crown. On hearing of the shipwreck, William had Harold brought to Rouen and refused to let him leave until he'd sworn on holy relics that he would support William's claim to the English throne. Later Harold maintained that this oath did not count, excusing himself on the grounds that it was forced from him.

In 1065, the dying Edward the Confessor named Harold as his successor, breaking his promise to William. Harold knew that William would be furious and so had himself crowned in January 1066, the day after the king died. William believed Harold had taken what was rightfully his, breaking a sacred oath into the bargain. The stage was set for war.

William gathered his barons and prepared for an invasion. A fleet of seven hundred ships carrying five thousand infantry and three thousand knights set sail from Normandy on 27 September 1066. They landed the next day near the old Roman fort of Pevensey Bay and then marched to Hastings, where William established a camp and waited for Harold to arrive.

Unfortunately for Harold, his men had been fighting another claimant to the English throne – Harald Hardraada of Norway – in the north of England, and after the long march to Hastings his men were exhausted.

Fighting started on 14 October 1066. Before the battle, William reminded his soldiers they had never lost under his command, then bravely led the first charge. Three horses are said to have been killed from under him during this one day. At one point during the fierce battle, a rumour spread that he had been killed. William removed his helmet to prove that he was alive and then hurled himself forward, killing several more English fighters.

By late afternoon the Normans clearly had the upper hand. When Harold was killed, the English admitted defeat. William was now King of England and was crowned at Westminster on Christmas Day.

After the Battle of Hastings, William ruthlessly crushed any English opponents and soon gained complete control of the country. He imposed order on a lawless land. An Englishman at the time wrote admiringly, "any honest man could travel over his kingdom without injury with his bosom full of gold, and no one dared strike another, however much wrong he had done him".

Throughout his long life William remained steadfastly loyal to his mother's family and the people who had supported him during his turbulent childhood. Nicholas was his leading churchman. His uncle, Walter, became a wealthy man. Odo, son of Herleve, and William's half-brother, was appointed Bishop of Bayeux and, after the invasion of England, acted as his brother's deputy, becoming Earl of Kent and acquiring immense estates scattered in the south and east of England. Robert, Herleve's youngest son, was also given vast tracts of land, including most of Cornwall and a section of Yorkshire.

William died on 9 September 1087, at the grand age of sixty, after suffering an internal injury caused by a horse rearing and ramming the pommel of his saddle into his stomach. His death was long, drawn out and painful; however, it did allow him time to settle his affairs. Normandy was left to Robert, his eldest child, while England was left to his second son – the future King William II. William is said to have confessed to his sins and asked in particular to be forgiven for the great loss of life he had caused during his many battles.

William's body was transported to Caen for burial where it was met by a distinguished band of mourners, including the aged abbot, Nicholas of Saint-Ouen. However, his funeral was marred by a macabre incident. During the service, a fire broke out in the town. After the fire was exhausted, the ceremony was hurriedly concluded. However, the pallbearers struggled to cram the king's bloated corpse into his stone coffin. The body split, creating a hideous smell and driving many mourners from the cathedral.

Even then, William found little peace. The tomb of the great warrior has been disturbed several times. It was rifled in 1562, when his remains were scattered and, lost, with the exception of a single thigh bone. This was reburied under an elaborate monument which was later destroyed in 1793 during the French Revolution. Today only a simple stone plaque marks the place where William was buried.

William's invasion changed British society in a manner which is still evident today. He built many of Britain's great castles, including Dover, Windsor and the Tower of London. French, the language of the Normans, mixed with Old English to create the modern, richer English language now spoken round much of the world. Many of England's great land-owning families are descended from invading Norman nobles, and the British Royal family can trace its bloodline, admittedly tenuously, back over almost a thousand years to the last man to successfully invade the island – William the Conqueror.

AUTHOR'S NOTES

When I first began to research the early years of William the Conqueror's life, I found that there is very little detail before the decisive battle with Cotentin and Guy at Val-es-Dunes in 1047. Historians' knowledge of his whereabouts during the first twelve years of his dukedom is sketchy as this period was so turbulent. However, there are some records to draw on, including Norman charters and the written testimonies of historians, often monks, working at the time or in the following century.

When writing this story I have tried to make sure that I have included the historical facts that are recorded and the key characters in William's early life. Duke Robert did go to Jerusalem, leaving his young bastard son in the care of King Henry of France, and William was knighted by the French king at some stage in his teenage years. William did take refuge on the Island of Vaudreuil, is likely to have met Edward the Confessor and did support his return to England. The guardians that Duke Robert appointed – Gilbert and Osbern – were both killed in quick succession in the early 1040s, Gilbert being assassinated and Osbern murdered in William's bedroom. Thereafter the duke's life became particularly precarious.

A monk historian writing in the twelfth century tells us that he was often in danger and that Walter, his mother's brother, hid him for safety in the houses of the poor. A Norman bard wrote poetry describing William's epic solitary ride from Valognes to King Henry of France, the battle of Val-es-Dunes and the knight Tesson's defection from Guy to William.

Although these facts are agreed, I have, of course, had to imagine the characters of the main players. We do have some clues from the past. Nicholas remained loyal to William throughout the duke's long reign. He was a learned monk who was abbot of the famous Saint-Ouen monastery for over fifty years. Duke Robert was much feared and was known by his nickname, "Robert the Devil". Guy turned against his own cousin, and Gacé came to the duke's rescue at a crucial time. Finally, William is described in a number of historical sources as being unusually tall, burly but not ungainly, and his exceptional physical strength is often noted. Only one painting, copied many times through the ages, survives. It shows a large, intimidating king with russet hair. Of his personal character we also have some evidence. He is frequently portrayed as a fluent and persuasive speaker and is described as physically brave. His tumultuous childhood appears to have given him the strength and ruthless self-belief to re-establish the Normans as the dominant force in France, and to lead his men in the successful invasion of England.

NOTES ABOUT THE PAST

CASTLES: Early Norman castles were built from wood. Earth was dug up to create a mound with a flat top, called a motte. A simple wooden tower was built on the motte for the lord and his family, and surrounded by a fence. The bailey was a courtyard at the base of the motte, containing many buildings for craftsmen and servants.

By the time of William the Conqueror, the Normans had begun to switch from wood to stone. Many of these stone castles survive today, including Ely, Durham, the Tower of London and Windsor (in England), and Caen, Mont-Saint-Michel and Falaise (in France).

KNIGHTS: Norman knights were the best trained and equipped soldiers in Europe. Training began when a boy was seven years old. He would become a page to a lord and learn how to ride, fight, and use a sword and bow. At fourteen he would become a squire and ride into battle with his master. Only if he proved himself brave and loyal would he be knighted. This happened at a dubbing ceremony where he would be hit by his master. A form of this ceremony still survives today – rather than strike a knight, the British monarch now taps him or her gently with a sword.

HUNTING: In Medieval times, hunting was seen as excellent training for battle. Chasing behind hounds or shooting cornered deer with arrows developed the skills of manoeuvring a horse at speed and hitting moving targets.

William the Conqueror's lifelong love of hunting was legendary. In Hampshire he cleared 150 square miles of land, people and villages for his sport, creating the New Forest. This royal playground is still preserved today as an English national park.

WRITING: Very few Normans could read or write. This was regarded as a skill necessary only for monks and priests. There were no printing presses and so any letters or books – mainly the Bible and other religious works – were laboriously copied onto paper or vellum using quill pens in a style of writing known as calligraphy.

HEALTH: In Norman times most people suffered from chronic ill health and life expectancy was short. This was due to poor diet and living conditions. Most people lived in one-room hovels with a central fire whose choking soot caused lung disease. Even large castles were draughty and damp, and mildew was an everyday occurrence. People frequently suffered from illnesses such as scurvy, skin and eye complaints, and rickets. Physical disfigurements were also much more commonplace than they are today.

MEDICINE: Medieval doctors had little understanding of basic hygiene, human anatomy or infection control. Instead medieval physicians believed that the body was built from four elements known as 'humours' – black bile, phlegm, blood and yellow bile. Illnesses were believed to be caused when these humours were out of balance. To correct the balance, doctors would bleed their patients using leeches, cuts or cups.

RELIGION: During Norman times, the church had a pervasive influence on people's lives, and bishops and archbishops were powerful men, often living at court.

Many of the Norman beliefs appear very superstitious to us today. They believed in the power of relics, that a comet heralded disaster and that a perjurer, someone who lied under oath, would die from a weapon in the eye. This might be the reason that Harold is depicted in the Bayeux Tapestry with just such an injury.

RELICS: Medieval Christians had a strong belief in the power of relics – the physical remains of a holy site or a holy person, such as fragments of a saint's bone, hair and teeth, and pieces from Christ's cross and clothes. Relics were believed to be responsible for miracles and had healing powers. They also added particular significance to an oath. It was for this reason that William insisted that Harold swear on a saint's relics when he promised to support the Norman duke's claim to the English throne.

TRUCE OF GOD: A Truce of God was a decree that forbade fighting at certain times. It was used in the medieval era to try to control knights in areas blighted by continual fighting. The pronouncement came with the blessing of the church, and it was for the church to enforce. Bishops and priests did this by excommunicating anyone who broke the truce, meaning that they could not attend mass or expect salvation in the afterlife. In a religious age this was a severe punishment.

William's Truce of God was one of the earliest of its kind. It was unusual as the ban against private war did not apply to him or his men. This gave him a significant advantage over his nobles and allowed him to mop up the last of the rebels and assert his authority over Normandy.

THE BAYEUX TAPESTRY: The conquest of England by William the Conqueror was famously depicted by the Bayeux Tapestry, sewn in England and completed some eleven years after the famous battle. It measures 50 centimetres by 70 metres (20 inches by 230 feet) and is a unique visual document of the Battle of Hastings and events leading up to the Norman invasion.

THE DOMESDAY BOOK: In 1085, two years before his death, William ordered that more information on England, "how it was occupied, and with what sort of people", be collected. The result was the Domesday Book, one of Britain's earliest public records. This book describes in remarkable detail the land and resources of much of rural England twenty years after the invasion. It is one of the earliest legal documents and is preserved in the National Archives in London.

The Domesday Book was originally called "The Winchester Book", as Winchester was the first Norman seat of government in Britain. It acquired its strange nickname because the English likened it to the Christian Day of Judgment – the Doomsday; there was no right of appeal against its records, which determined the level of tax payable.

Before they were famous ... meet Cleopatra, who will one day be the Queen of Egypt, in this new series about the early lives of some of history's most charismatic figures.

A young girl flees the city, fearing for her life. Living in hiding, uncertain of her future, she finally receives news from home. The time has come to face her enemies – and take her place as Princess Cleopatra, future Queen of Egypt.

"The focus is on providing factual information within an historical context that gives a flavour of the times while delivering a first-rate story." Publishing News

BY CAROLINE CORBY

Before they were famous ... meet Boudica, one day to be England's warrior queen, in this new series about the early lives of some of history's most charismatic figures.

In Ancient Britain, a tribesman's daughter is in trouble. The Romans have invaded, her father has been accused of murder and she doesn't know who to trust. When a mysterious druid appears in her village, she knows she must enter his murky world if she is to bring honour to her tribe and one day become Boudica, warrior queen.

BY CAROLINE CORBY

Before they were famous ... meet Pocahontas, a young Native American girl who saved the first English colony in Virginia and shaped the destiny of her people for ever, in this new series about the early lives of some of history's most charismatic figures.

There was a prophecy talked of amongst the Powhatan tribe – a prophecy that one day a nation would spring from Chesapeake Bay and destroy them. When ships land there, Chief Powhatan wants the intruders killed. Pocahontas bravely intervenes and persuades her father to befriend the foreigners. But are they to be trusted or will the prophecy come true? Pocahontas learns that bringing two cultures together comes at a cost.

BY CAROLINE CORBY